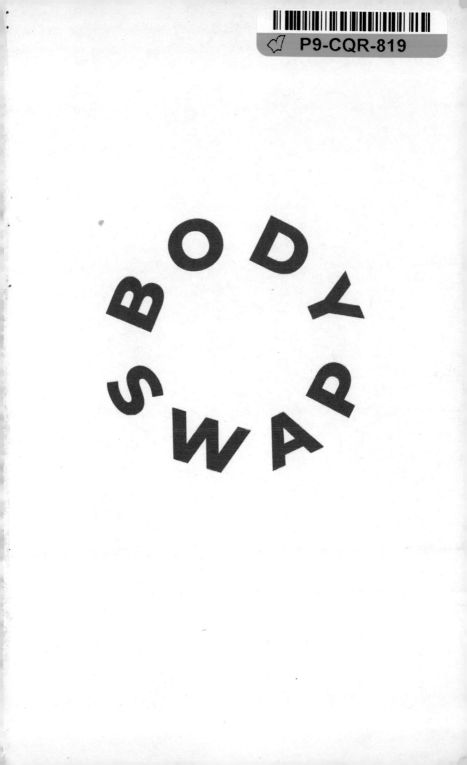

BODY SWAP

SYLVIA MCNICOLL

DUNDURN
TORONTO

Cover image: istock.com/Vertyr
Printer: Webcom

Library and Archives Canada Cataloguing in Publication

McNicoll, Sylvia, 1954-, author
    Body swap / Sylvia McNicoll.

Issued in print and electronic formats.
ISBN 978-1-4597-4090-7 (softcover).--ISBN 978-1-4597-4091-4 (PDF).--
ISBN 978-1-4597-4092-1 (EPUB)

    I. Title.

PS8575.N52B63 2018   jC813'.54   C2017-907854-2
                                               C2017-907855-0

1 2 3 4 5   22 21 20 19 18

We acknowledge the support of the **Canada Council for the Arts**, which last year invested $153 million to bring the arts to Canadians throughout the country, and the **Ontario Arts Council** for our publishing program. We also acknowledge the financial support of the **Government of Ontario**, through the **Ontario Book Publishing Tax Credit** and the **Ontario Media Development Corporation**, and the **Government of Canada**.

Nous remercions le **Conseil des arts du Canada** de son soutien. L'an dernier, le Conseil a investi 153 millions de dollars pour mettre de l'art dans la vie des Canadiennes et des Canadiens de tout le pays.

Care has been taken to trace the ownership of copyright material used in this book. The author and the publisher welcome any information enabling them to rectify any references or credits in subsequent editions.

— *J. Kirk Howard, President*

VISIT US AT

dundurn.com | @dundurnpress | dundurnpress | dundurnpress

Dundurn
3 Church Street, Suite 500
Toronto, Ontario, Canada
M5E 1M2

For my readers, always, and especially for my nine grands:
Hunter, William, Jadzia, Violet, Desmond, Fletcher,
Finley, Scarlett, and Ophelia, who make the privilege
of growing old so much greater

CHAPTER 1

The Accident

"THAT CELLPHONE WILL KILL YOU!" a raspy voice warns. It comes from someone standing in front of me on the bus. Someone who smells like dirty socks and stale coffee. A male voice that sounds very definite about phone fatalities.

I ignore him. What's happening on my little screen is way more important.

Megan is texting me about Chael Caruso, the boy whose name is written in big loops all over the inside cover of my journal, together with mine, of course. *Chael loves Hallie. Mrs. Chael Prince-Caruso, Hallie and Chael forever.* That one's in a heart with an arrow through it.

And today, we're finally going to begin our forever.

A cane knocks hard into my knee. "Ow!" Does the old guy plan to beat me to death with that thing? He coughs a loud fake *ahem, ahem.*

Seniors' day at the mall. Why do they have to have it during *our* Christmas break? The stuffy warm bus heats up all the body odours into a boiled-broccoli-and-wet-dog potpourri. Makes me hot and irritable. I ignore him and lean toward my best friend, Abby, who is sitting on a window seat facing forward.

On the right side of her face, Abby's hair angles to a pale blue arrow; the left is shaved close, making her look like a techno angel. She alone understands the importance of what's happening on my phone right now and raises one blond eyebrow in a question mark.

I continue typing.

Did you ask Chael if he likes me? I press send. The answer to that text could potentially cheer me back up. Chael (pronounced Kale, yet nothing like the vegetable) has coffee-coloured eyes and smooth maple skin. A smile that's as wide as a soccer field. He's centre forward for our junior team, same position I play on the girls' team. Our babies could be soccer stars. I sigh.

When I finally lift my eyes from the screen, I see the crepey blue-veined hand that grips the hook of the cane that hit me. Above the knuckles, blue, loopy letters spell *Carpe Diem*. My eyes raise higher to his face. Watery grey eyes stare back at me, expecting something. What? With the light from the window, his hair glows a bright silver.

Abby gives me a hard stare, too. "Hallie!" She punches my shoulder.

"What?"

"Give him your seat!"

I don't get it. There are thirty other places available; I don't know why he wants this particular one on the front bench facing the centre aisle. Giving it up will mean I can't talk to Abby as easily because she's wedged in beside a lady with a walker. That woman smells like lily of the valley; the sweetness of it squeezes at my throat. Dirty socks and lilies, what a combo. *Gahh!*

"If only I had a car," I grumble to Abby as I rise from the bench and try to shuffle around the old guy.

"And could drive." Abby grins, a braces-dazzling grin.

"I drive the truck on Uncle Bill's farm."

"And your licence then."

"My birthday's in April. Fast as I can get it, we will be out of here." My phone interrupts with a belch, which is how it signals incoming texts and calls. *Megan!* I check to see what she's answered. Her words will be crucial to who the father of my babies will be, and I want seven, just like the Von Trapps in *The Sound of Music*. Strange maybe, but that's our family's favourite Christmas movie.

This could be the best Christmas present ever. A cool boyfriend. Holding hands, kissing at our lockers. Smiling, happy. High school sweethearts, we'll tell our seven kids later.

I sigh again. The bus lurches forward and I tumble against the man who stabs my foot with his cane this time.

"Ow!" I call out and glare.

"See what I mean ..." he says, the tiniest bit of a smile lifting up his thin lips, "about cellphones?"

"It's your cane that's a lethal weapon!" I grumble and read the screen as I scootch into the seat behind Abby. "Oh, yay! *Yesss!*" Leaning forward, I tell Abby, "Megan says Chael likes me!"

"Told ya!"

"But he called me thunder thighs at indoor soccer the other day." I shake my head at the message on the tiny screen.

"You're such a great kicker. He's probably talking about the power in your thigh muscles ..."

"Nah, I think he means I'm fat."

"You may *have* fat but *you* are not fat," Abby continues, "just pleasantly round."

I grab my face with my free hand. It's shaped like a soccer ball, no cheekbones poking through at all. And I've conditioned my hair into gentle curls, but they soften my jawline, make me look pudgy. And I'm short — if my legs were longer, they'd look leaner.

Like Abby's. I glance over at her skinny-jeaned legs. No thunder happening there. She has great bones anyway, a strong chin and cheekbones. I grip my forehead. "Oh no!"

"What's wrong?"

Just above my eyebrows, my fingers find one of those hard bumps. I push down on it and it hurts. "A zit!"

"Never mind. We're here."

The bus begins to pull into the right lane.

Suddenly, the driver leans on her horn and brakes.

One of those new Hurricane SUVs shoots around the bus. It's as red and shiny as a polished apple. I smile at it. Such a cool car! "Someday, I'm going to drive one of those," I tell Abby.

"Me too. We'll race them."

I grin and shrug. "Probably need to save till we're a hundred."

The bus slows to the stop. I stand up before Lily of the Valley can move her walker, but not fast enough to beat the guy with the cane. He blocks me and takes forever to shuffle forward.

Another belch comes from my cellphone. I look at the screen: *Chael and Hardeep are hanging out at the food court.* "Oh my gosh. What am I going to do? He's here too!" I touch the zit on my forehead. It seems to have doubled in size.

"Leave it alone! You're making it worse." Abby motions as if to slap my hand down, but the woman with the walker stands between us.

Down the stairs I go behind the guy with silver hair moving ever so *s-l-o-w-l-y.* I text as my feet go down. *What exactly did Chael say about me?*

In the middle of the steps, the old dude stops to pull on a red woollen hat, but I don't notice till I bump into him.

He turns and frowns at me. "You are going to miss out on so much of life if you don't put that thing away."

"Sorr-*eeee.*" If only he would move. Quicker. Come on! I want to push him out of the way. I'm missing out on so much of life 'cause of *him*! Could have texted a Harry Potter novel by now. I finally press send. I need to catch up with Chael.

Or do I? Do I want him to see me like this? With this pumpkin in the middle of my forehead? Another belch and the old man turns to give me a look.

"It's not me, it's my phone," I tell him and read the latest text.

Chael says you're funny.

Finally, we're off the bus. As I stumble forward, I key into my phone: *Funny ha ha or funny weird?*

Abby follows close behind and bumps against me. "Move it, Hallie, if you want to see Chael before he leaves."

But maybe I don't. I'm funny. Is he just messing with me? His eyes do always look at me like they're laughing.

We climb through the snowbank edging the parking lot, and my sneakers get buried instantly. This will be the first white Christmas we've had in a long time, but it's still fairly warm and I'm in winter-boot denial. I lift my feet out of the sticky white and we continue toward the mall.

Squish, squish, my sneakers slog along. "Can we stop at the drug mart? I wouldn't mind picking up some concealer for this." I point to my forehead.

Abby rolls her eyes. "Then we'll miss them for sure."

A burp sounds again.

"Look at it later." Abby keeps going.

But my fingers itch; I can't help myself, I have to see what Megan has to say. Dropping back, I lift the phone closer to my face.

"Hallie!" Abby calls.

I start to run as I read. *Chael's leaving Doughnut Time. Where are you?*

"Hallie! Hallie!" Abby calls.

I run without looking up. We can still make it. We'll skip the cosmetics department.

Abby's voice turns strangely high-pitched. "Watch out!"

Whomp! A hard force explodes into me.

Time slows down as I get hurled into the air. My cellphone flies from my hand, and I watch it cartwheel through the air, then crash on the ice and shatter into pieces right next to the red Hurricane that hit me.

Then I slam onto the iced pavement headfirst. A coconut cracks and pain splinters into a million scalding-white lights somewhere behind my eyes.

Hot, hot, my head feels like it's on fire with white pain. Then cooler, cooler, shivering … I'm cold. I lie still as, bit by bit, my body and mind shake loose of each other.

I hear Abby crying, loud at first. "Hallie, no! Hallie! Someone call 911." But her voice becomes more and more distant.

I can hear myself breathing. *In … out … in.* Something warm drips from my head, and it feels like the last drops of syrup letting go from the bottom of a bottle.

I see Abby's black-and-yellow shoes near my face; behind her legs, the dented red bumper.

My breathing slows to a last gasp; it doesn't seem necessary anymore. Instead, I feel myself lifting, floating, a helium balloon suddenly dancing and free. Below me I see my body sprawled on the snow, a white boxy ER truck, and a woman on a stretcher. Faded yellowy hair and a pale, white wrinkled face with a blue tinge. *She* was the driver? A hot bitter thought scalds me. *She's too old to be driving.* My vision fills with a liquid black.

CHAPTER 2

The Swap

MUSIC TINKLES BRIGHT AND CHEERFUL as I open my eyes. A breeze blows soft and warm against my skin, no winter bite to it. I scramble to my feet to find I'm wearing flip-flops instead of sneakers, shorts instead of jeans, and my favourite yellow happy-face T-shirt. No winter jacket. Oh no, did I miss Christmas?

Screams pierce the air. But they're energetic and happy. Not sudden and horrified — the kind of reaction you'd get to, say, an accident in a parking lot. Maybe it was all a dream.

I smell hot dogs and popcorn and inhale deeply. Mmm! There's also a hint of sweetness — cotton candy? Yes, that's it. Carnival smells! It has to be. I smile. Travelling carnivals are my favourite, the coloured lights, the happy children and hand-holding lovers, all the junky foods, the music and screams, and the swirling, dizzying rides, especially the roller coaster. I look around for one but instead see a carousel in front of me. White unicorns with blue flowers on their bridles gallop up and down. I blink and see an assortment of people riding them: an overweight man in a suit, a spindly looking granny, and a teenaged girl. Sitting in the chariots behind them, a mom holds her baby, a couple lean against each other. Not as many kids as you would expect. They all smile but look distant. As they go around, I swear I can see the sunlight coming through them. Mirrors cover the centre of the carousel, but the people are not reflected in them.

Maybe this is a dream.

Where's the roller coaster? I wonder as I walk around to the mad teacup ride. It's empty and stopped, so I figure I'll try that instead.

The operator appears from out of nowhere, grinning. "Step right up!" He offers me his hand, palm up.

"Um, where do I buy a ticket?" I ask, looking him in the eyes.

"You already bought it." He pushes back long brown bangs from his eyes, which are bright blue and sparkle like a brook. Young eyes in weathered skin. Laughing, laughing. Who does he remind me of? He winks as he grabs my hand and leads me to a large yellow cup. No one else sits in any of the other of the teacups, so I expect him to wait till the ride draws more people.

Only he never does. The cups jerk to a start, swirling around each other.

As the cups circle faster and faster, I begin to see people in them, my uncle Leo, our last mayor, and is that Gord Downie? Why are they all here? The light shines through them, too.

It comes to me finally. They're all dead. The thought

makes me queasy and I look down at my arm. It's looking a bit, well, transparent.

The ride stops abruptly.

"Where are my manners? You don't like teacup parties, you like adrenalin thrills," the operator says.

How would he know? But something does seem very familiar about him. That something floats loose in my mind as I reach for it. Not the way he looks but more the glint in his eyes, his mannerisms. He holds out his hand and I see it in a flash. The tattoo.

Carpe Diem! "You're the guy from the bus! But that's impossible! You're too young."

"You got me dead to rights. Heh-heh! The name's Eli."

"Oh my God, you're a shape-shifter."

"You had it right the first time."

"What do you mean?"

"What you said." He waits for a moment.

I think that over. Then it hits me. *Oh my God.* My face grows hot. Eli means he is God.

Even though I haven't said anything, he nods and smiles. Then he tugs my hand. "Follow me."

I resist for a moment. Plant my feet, refuse to move. I should wake up any moment.

"Come on. You want to continue on your journey, don't you?" He pulls harder.

My feet stutter along the pavement as I try to slow us down. "Where's Abby?" I ask. "My best friend," I add, as though I need to explain. But he would know that, wouldn't he?

"She didn't step in front of an SUV."

My feet continue moving forward but my stomach wants to heave.

"I warned you not to keep staring at that itty-bitty screen. Told you that you'd miss out on life."

We approach a huge wooden roller coaster. I've never seen one made out of wood. Is it safe?

My eyes follow the rails of the ride. There's one hill and another. The final one rises high up into the clouds and disappears. "This has to be some kind of nightmare."

"More like a good dream. A very long one. You like roller coasters, don't you? Step aboard." He flings open a wooden gate.

"I ... I don't feel like it. I can't go on alone." I look around for someone to help me.

"Well, if you just wait a moment, someone will be along shortly to join you." He looks to the side of me expectantly.

Something shimmers in the air and I watch, hypnotized. Just like that moment when my cellphone spun around in the air, time slows down. A tall silhouette forms and fills in, becoming an older woman. She fusses with her faded blond hair and looks beyond me to the roller coaster. "My, my." She smiles. "I haven't been on one of these in years. Didn't think they still made them like this."

"Well, they're making a comeback," Eli says.

The face and hair look familiar. Oh my God. She's the woman from the stretcher. I shake my finger at her. "You're the one who hit me with your car."

"Be sweet," Eli suggests. "You wanted a partner for the ride."

"I can't go on with her!"

"Why not? Roller coasters are her favourite, too. You have so much in common."

"That's all right, dear," the older woman's voice soothes. "My son Ron was afraid of them, too."

"I'm not scared of roller coasters. But if we get on this ride, you know we'll never come back!"

"Oh now, *back* is so overrated. Why would I want to return to a life full of achy joints and shaky fingers?" Suddenly she throws her arms open wide. "Life is a highway, I want to ride it all night long!"

She's so happy, it's annoying. "Stop singing! Don't you have a family?"

"Certainly — I have a son who thinks I'm a bother and a daughter and a couple of grandchildren out west who hardly know me anymore."

"Well, bully for you. I've never even kissed a boy." I curl my hands into fists. "Now I never will. And it's all your fault."

"I was backing out. You stepped behind the car," she says calmly.

"You should have braked!" I shriek at her.

"I did. The accelerator stuck."

"You just confused the pedals. People your age shouldn't drive!"

"Why didn't you watch where you were going? Young people are always in a hurry!"

"I was running to catch up with a hot guy from school. Who *likes* me." I hold up my thumb and forefinger. "I was this close to getting a boyfriend."

"With a cellphone in front of your face."

"Ladies, ladies!" Eli holds up his hands like stop signs. "All that is history. Why don't you just have some fun together?"

"Because what she said is not true — you know it's not," the older woman argues. "And it's what everyone will say. Even my own son. I had the car in for the acceleration problem. The stupid mechanic said it was the floor mat and my boots. And I was wearing athletic runners!"

Eli shakes his head. "You can't get quality workmanship these days."

Her face turns pink; her eyes burn at him.

I'd like to hit him just as much as the old lady does. "I don't care. I just want to kiss a guy before I die. Is that too much to ask?"

"Well, I *do* care! I lived a good life and don't want the ending to be smirched."

"Smirched?" I repeat.

"You know, that everyone blames me for killing you."

So I am dead. Of course, I suspected as much.

Eli turns from me to the lady and back again. He doesn't look as smug anymore so I press the issue.

"You run this whole carnival; you can change things. This accident. Give us both another chance." That last line comes out sounding desperate; I change tactics, and my voice. "What do you say? The old lady and I can have fun together and prove her case while we're alive."

"Susan … the name is Susan MacMillan not 'old lady' or 'her.' And you are?"

"Hallie Prince. I'd like to say that I'm pleased to meet you."

"But under these circumstances, how can you be? Really … Eli, is it?" Susan turns to the carnival operator. "The Hurricane is a dangerous car. More people will be injured and killed if Saji Motors doesn't find the flaw and fix it. With Hallie's help, perhaps I can get someone to listen."

Eli nods thoughtfully. Then he grins, maybe too energetically.

I'm not sure I trust his excitement.

"All right Susan and Hallie. You don't have to ride the roller coaster yet if you don't like. You're both going to have your different ending. More different than you can ever imagine."

CHAPTER 3

Hallie

MY EYES FLUTTER OPEN. I STARE AT a dashboard, the top of a steering wheel pressed to my forehead. This can't be. I don't even have a driver's licence. Around my chest a band of steel feels like it's tightening. "Ow, ow, ow!"

Someone taps at the window.

"Reach into that purse and get a nitroglycerine pill," a voice orders.

"A what?" I don't have a purse, and whose car am I in anyways? Mom drives a minivan. I turn my head and see the old man from the bus. Not the carnival operator. "Eli?"

It's his cane tapping. "Open up and I'll help you."

My head lifts. I struggle with the buttons to unlock the car door and he does the rest: opens the door, reaches across me, fumbles through a blue leather bag, unscrews a vial, and shakes out a round white pill. "Place this under your tongue." He sticks his fingers in my mouth, so I don't have a choice.

Bleh, yuck, old man fingers.

"Don't swallow it or it won't work."

The pill tastes bitter and sends a sharp, burning sensation through my head.

"Take deep breaths," Eli tells me.

I inhale and the steel band starts to loosen. My head feels full, my face warm.

"Is it better yet?"

I nod. "A little."

"Then come talk to Hallie. See how she's doing and apologize."

"What are you talking about? I'm Hallie."

"Well, yes and no. Your soul belongs to you, so yes. But your body is all Susan. And people do tend to judge by covers. So no."

"Don't be ridiculous." But as I flip down the makeup mirror, I notice the skin on my hand is pale. Between brown spots and blue, bulgy veins, that is. I gasp.

"Relax. You've just had a bout with angina. You shouldn't have any more shocks."

Too late. My lips are thin, my eyes blue and watery with purple circles underneath them. Wrinkles roadmap from the corners of my eyes and mouth. Not only am I white, I'm ancient! I breathe faster. "No!" I scream. Across my forehead is a curved band of violet — a steering-wheel bruise forming.

"On the plus side, remember how you've always wanted to lose weight?"

My hands slap down to long, thin thighs. My knees feel knobby and they throb. I'm hyperventilating.

"Easy, breathe out. Nice and slow." He puts his hand on my back.

I close my eyes. It takes me a while to open them again.

"There now. That's better."

"You think this is a great joke, don't you? Well, ha-ha on me. I've learned my lesson: it sucks to be old. Now switch me back."

He shakes a crooked finger at me. "But you haven't proven Susan innocent."

"That's because she isn't! Come on. That was just me bargaining with you to get some more life. I never really believed her."

"Exactly." Eli taps the hood a couple of times. "Go over to her. Help her up."

"Her? She's in my body?"

"Yes," Eli whispers. "Remember, you look like Susan now. Don't let on you're not."

I stare at him but don't see even a trace of a smile. "Or what? Something worse will happen?"

He shrugs. "People will think you're suffering from dementia. Put you in an old-age home." He claps his hand over mine and squeezes. "This is your one chance."

"My one chance to be old?"

He tilts his head and lifts his chin. "Growing old is a privilege — one *you* may not even earn." He raises his white-cloud eyebrows.

I sigh and swivel my body toward the open door. I lift my legs over to the outside. When I stand up, one knee feels like it's going to collapse, but Eli grabs my elbow and hands me the blue purse. Then he leans on his cane as, together, we hobble over the snow to my former body, now Susan's.

Abby crouches close to her, calling to her and crying.

When I reach them, I stop and wring my hands. "Oh, I'm so dreadfully sorry." *Dreadfully* — that's a word old ladies use, isn't it? "I didn't see her. Is she all right?"

Abby shakes her head and sobs. "I don't know. She's not answering me."

CHAPTER 4

Susan

MY BACK, OH IT'S SO COLD ... ICE ... parking lot ... why am I lying on the hard ground? I must get up or I'll catch my death. But I need to move slowly, don't want my sciatica to act up.

"Hallie, Hallie!" Someone shakes my shoulder.

Stop that! My head aches and feels as though it's filled with a hot fog. Dementia? Has it finally set in? *Calm down,* I scold myself. It's no sin; one in five after eighty succumb to Alzheimer's, and I celebrated that birthday two years ago. I force my eyelids apart.

A face hovers in front of me, blurry, with blue hair, badly cut. I blink again, surely a vision. Some strange-looking angel.

She addresses me. "Are you okay, Hallie?"

I remember now. Hallie is the name of that girl I met at the carnival. The one who stepped behind my car as I was backing up. Perhaps this hovering face belongs to a friend of hers? Someone should fix that haircut; it's unfortunate, hacked too short on one side. Or are my eyes playing tricks on me?

"Talk to me, please!"

Blessed Mary, will she never stop bleating? How can a person think? I push myself up on my hands, waiting for my wrists to answer in pain. But they don't ache at all, nor do my fingers or palms. It was easy! I look down at them, and that's when I notice. My heart thumps hard. I'm black!

Calm down, I tell myself a second time. My skin is lovely, young and smooth. And the extra pigment is so practical and protective. I have to say, I like the new me.

All my life I've been pasty white. My mother used to slather me with baby oil and tell me to sit out in the sun so I could get some colour. Unfortunately, that colour was always red, and then later the skin would tighten and crack into white flakes. Mother is long dead, but once a year, these days, I visit the dermatologist so he can burn off my pre-cancer cells.

But enough delay. I'm definitely going to attempt standing now. I wriggle my toes first and stretch my legs. It's the only way to warm up my joints and get the circulation flowing. Otherwise, I will hobble like the little old lady I never wanted to be. When exactly did I grow so old?

As I move to a crouch, I realize my knees and ankles don't hurt at all, nor do my Achilles tendons.

"Hallie, Hallie!"

I take a breath. My name is Susan, I'm certain of it. Not Hallie. And I will smack her one if she shakes my shoulder again. Oh, but I mustn't. I can't say anything, either; I must play along. Since I turned eighty, I find they're always looking for ways to point out how stupid I am.

The veil of fog lifts and I peer down at my legs. They're so different, shorter, rounder, and I'm wearing jeans. Farmers' pants, totally unsuitable to wear shopping. I scramble up the rest of the way and feel the strength in my leg muscles, which can't possibly belong to me. I want to jump up and down to enjoy them, but then I notice my old body standing beside the blue-haired girl.

"I'm dreadfully sorry I hit you. Are you hurt?" That's my voice coming from my body.

But I touch my lips; they haven't moved, and they feel different too, softer, fuller. "No," I answer, "I feel better than I have for a long time."

And it's true. Even my new voice sounds smooth and energetic. I smile.

An older gentleman stands next to my former body. I've seen him sometimes at the local deli. There's always been something odd about him, a strength and confidence that most seniors do not project.

He's holding my former elbow and I see the tattoo. *Carpe Diem*, "seize the day," if my Latin serves me. Just like that carnival operator, Eli. Then it strikes me, hard as a baseball bat.

Eli means God in Hebrew. Can it be?

"But that car really threw you, Hallie!" The strange angel keeps calling me by that other girl's name, and from the parts of my body that I can see, I now look like Hallie.

Eli warned us about different endings.

"And you're holding your head," she continues.

Instantly, I drop my hand. If I am in her body, is Hallie in mine? Did Eli mean he would switch our bodies?

"Maybe you have a concussion," the blue-haired angel says. "We need to get you to a hospital."

At the word *hospital*, I panic. "No, no!" My friend Margret's husband went in there with just a mild case of pneumonia but he came out in a box. "You can't send me there. I'll catch the *C. difficile* virus and die."

"What are you talking about? You've never been in a hospital before. Not even when you were born."

Too late, I see Eli tapping his nose, raising an eyebrow, signalling me.

Why? I've said something wrong? *Ohhh*, it dawns on me. My wariness of hospitals, not something a teen would necessarily have yet.

"Maybe the young lady is confused, give her a moment," Eli suggests.

"You probably read about germs and hospitals on the internet for a school project," says the person in my body. She is trying to help me. She's in on it. She has to be Hallie.

What a nightmare this must be for her, to be trapped in an octogenarian body.

"Ye-yes," I stammer. "*C. difficile* is something we learned about in class."

"Must have been when I was away then," Blue Hair says. "'Cause I sure don't remember."

"Perhaps you weren't paying attention," I snap. *Really, leave it alone, missy!* I watch as my old body bends to pick up the pieces of Hallie's cellphone from the ice. Even after dying and reincarnating into a senior, Hallie's first concern seems to be her phone. Too quickly, she straightens and a wave of pain passes over her face. I remember the feeling well.

"You may be fine," she tells me, "but your cellphone is toast." She grips her back and winces. "I would love to replace it for you." Flames burn in her eyes as she smiles, cunningly.

Still bearing a grudge, I think. Maybe she can burn off my old cataracts with that laser stare of hers.

"It's the least I can do for you after running you down." There's iron in Hallie's voice. This teenager is quite likely looking for revenge.

Two can play at this game. I smile, too, with my soft, young lips. "That's all right. I've learned my lesson about staring at phones while walking across parking lots. I won't be using one anymore." I scramble the rest of the way to my feet.

"Oh, but I insist. In fact, I've decided to step out of the Dark Ages and buy one of those new phones they've just released, the El-Q, for myself. Maybe they'll give me a deal for two."

Glaring at her, I bend down easily and scoop up the backpack that fell when the car hit her. "I couldn't accept, really. Those models are far too expensive."

"Are you kidding me?" Her friend, the blue-haired angel, stands up from her crouch. "Take the El-Q. She owes you."

Oh, the young people today! They think the whole world owes them.

"You can probably get all your contacts off the memory card from this one." Hallie holds up a small piece of the cellphone. "What do you think, Abby?"

The blue-haired angel squints suspiciously at this old body asking her the question. "How do you know my name?"

Indeed, how would she? This young Blue Hair is a sharp thing; it's going to be difficult to pull the wool over those angel eyes.

Hallie's wrinkled face turns pink. "You told me, remember?"

"Um, actually, I don't. Maybe we should just go home right now." Blue-haired Abby shifts on her feet, clearly uncomfortable at the prospect of spending any more time with this strange senior. Her eyes scan from Hallie to me. "You should both probably lie down."

I could use some quiet time to sort this out, I think. But where is home? Where will I go if my body and voice belong to someone else?

"First you need an El-Q." Hallie nods and winks at me. "So we can stay in touch. You know, in case you find out you're injured later on."

She has a point about staying in touch, a really good one. We can't carry this off if we don't. "All right. Shall we go back to the mall?"

"Okay, well ..." Abby interrupts. "My mother just texted me about an appointment. I HAVE to go home. Right now," she adds.

"Wait! Should I drive you?" Hallie asks.

Just because she's in an older person's body, she thinks she's capable of chauffeuring. We'll see about that. I try to catch her eyes. So disconcerting because, of course, they're my old eyes. "Perhaps we should get those El-Qs first. Just the two of us. We have things we need to discuss."

Abby shakes her head. "I can catch the bus. I'm good."

"What about lunch first?" Hallie pipes in. "My treat for everyone. We can go to Perspectives."

"Oh no," I interrupt, "the food court would be fine." Perspectives must be the most expensive restaurant in Burlington. How much is this switch going to cost me? This young girl doesn't understand anything about money. About making it last till the end of your life because you won't ever earn anything more.

"No, I insist. I owe you a proper lunch, considering how much pain I've put you through."

"Well, not me," Abby says. "You guys have fun. I see my bus coming. Bye!"

Just as well. I can't keep up the ruse in front of Hallie's friend. Hallie's going to have to fill me in on her entire life. "Okay, see you later, Abby." I wave, happy to remember her name. Of late, I've been so bad with those. But the mind I'm using now is as sharp as a tack. So clever! I'm really going to enjoy this body swap. Perhaps a great deal more than Hallie.

CHAPTER 5

Hallie

"WHERE IS HE?" I TURN AROUND in the parking lot, searching for Eli, but the old dude has conveniently disappeared. "I want to know how long I'm stuck in" — I wave my hands over the old lady's body — "this."

Susan purses my lips, a strange kind of mouth move that I don't usually do. "I think we just have to make the best of things the way they are." Of course she would be okay with the whole deal.

"Well, you can't leave your car in the middle of the road. Better park it, so we can check out the mall," I suggest.

"I … I can't. I don't trust it … or myself. I feel shaky." She covers her mouth with her hand, another thing I don't do. So weird to watch.

"Oh, give me a break!"

"In your body, I'm too young, anyway."

"Fine, I'll do it." I reach into her purse for keys.

"Do you know how to drive?"

"Yeah. I drive my uncle's truck all the time. Not sure about how well I park, though. There's always so much room on the farm." I head to the driver's side and get in.

"Saji Hurricanes are easy," she says, sliding in beside me. "When they work properly, they park themselves."

"But it's a big car and there's hardly any room."

"What I mean is Saji vehicles parks themselves, literally. There's a park-assist feature. Cameras and sensors." She waves her hands, fluttery, old-people style but with my teenaged hands.

She mentioned something about the floor mat at the carnival before, so just in case, I bend down to make sure the mat is clear of the gas pedal. Then I turn on the engine. The dash lights up in bottle blue. Susan switches on the park feature for me. I watch as the screen displays three sides of the Hurricane. "Wow, didn't think you liked technology."

"I don't. My son Ron convinced me. He's a lawyer. A good one. His wife, Sheryl, insisted I give up my licence after my heart attack. He talked me into buying a car with extra safety features instead."

"What do I do now?"

"Just drive it in. It will beep if you're too close to any of the other cars."

"Rats, a Smart car just pulled into our spot."

"Christmas. People circle for hours for a space." Susan cranes her neck. "See that single line of cars at the back near the snowbank? One spot just opened."

"Parallel parking?" I ask.

"May take you all of thirty seconds. Get over there, before someone takes it."

She's right, I better hurry. I turn the wheel, put it in drive, and accelerate gently. Of course, there's no problem. I know my gas pedal from my brake, not like some senior citizens I know. I test it out to make sure, stop for a moment, then accelerate again. Once we get to the line, I pull up to the car ahead of the spot.

"Now put it in reverse, let the steering wheel go, and accelerate."

"You trust it to park like that?" Makes me wonder if she believes her own story.

"It's quite amazing. Just be gentle on the gas."

I push my foot down and magically it moves backward. "Weird." It's like some supernatural being has taken over driving the car.

Beep, beep!

"That's the signal you're in. So brake. Perfect."

"Accelerator works fine."

"This time. If it malfunctioned consistently, I would have no problem getting it attended to."

"Sure." I switch off the car and get out again. But I'm way slower than she is.

She power-marches through the snow toward the mall.

I struggle to keep up with her. "Slow down, will ya? My knee hurts." Just as I get the words out, there's a dip in the pavement and the ball of my right foot lands harder than I expect. I stumble. "Ow. Geez, I'm clumsy."

Rabbit-quick, she doubles back to catch me. "Sorry. That bad knee always throws me off balance. I'll walk slower. Here, hold on." She sticks out her elbow for me. "It will make things easier and you won't slip on the ice."

This is embarrassing, but I grab onto her for all my decrepit arm is worth. Nobody will know me, anyways.

When we get closer to the entrance, a man presses the wheelchair button and the door opens automatically for us. Hey, we could have opened that ourselves.

"Thank you," Susan says. She parts her lips to show an even row of perfect teeth.

Those used to be mine. Did I ever have a nice smile! I never realized that before. My lips were a full pink bow. I wiggle my older lips — they feel dry and cracked.

"Where is this store?" Susan asks me as we enter the building.

"See if you can't smell it." I inhale deeply and enjoy the electric-wire fragrance of technology. I love it.

"This way?" She points to the left.

"Yup." It isn't far and the bright lights shining from inside the IQ store out-flash all the others. The large, plate windows combined with the two blank white walls along the sides make it look bigger than it already is.

The store bustles with people, most sitting around high tables with assorted screens in front of them. Clerks in black pants and white lab coats circle, each of them with an El-Q in their hand. Along the back wall, screens flash IQ messages. *How can we make your purchase more pleasant?* And *When in doubt, reboot.* Images of upcoming new models appear underneath. A long, white bar stretches in front of the screen, and a row of customers sit patiently on stools, all waiting for a lab coat to pay attention to their problems.

The lab coat who approaches us is cute. His hair tufts up with some kind of product. He has a slightly down-turned smile and puppy-dog brown eyes that right now are paying all kinds of attention to Susan, even though I'm smiling at him with all my might.

Do I have hideous yellow teeth in this body? I poke my tongue around in my mouth. Do I even have all my teeth? Seems like it. I close my lips, anyways.

"My name's Van. Is there something I can help you with today?"

"Well, Van, we want to look at the very latest El-Q," I tell him, trying my best to sound adult.

"Certainly. Come over this way." He leads us to a table near the left wall. "These are all the models we have in right now."

"How much do they cost?" Susan asks as she looks them over.

He squints at her. Why should a teen care, after all? "It depends, miss, on the features and the size of memory you want, but this one" — he points to the screen closest to us — "runs about six hundred."

"What! For a phone?" Susan shrieks. She's definitely coming across too senior citizen.

Van's eyebrows jump and his head tilts. "This isn't a phone, it's the future. An OLED screen so it's super sharp and light. Face ID, wireless charging, a long-life battery. The true depth camera has optimal image stabilization — you can take phenomenal photos, even with selfies …"

"Can you make phone calls?" Susan asks.

She is so embarrassing.

Van smiles at her. "Sure you can." He shrugs. "But don't you just text?"

I cough to get his attention but his eyes never leave

Susan. He thinks she's cute, I can tell. In my body, she *is* cute! Cuteness gets attention power; I had power before. I never knew that. Now, in Susan's body, it's like I'm invisible.

"We'll take two, please." It comes out in a creaky old-lady voice. I hold my neck as I clear my throat. But, of course, that voice doesn't shock anyone else but me.

"No problem." Van instantly keys something into his own device. "Says here there are exactly two left in the back. Let me go see." He rushes away.

Once Van leaves, Susan hisses at me. "You can't use up all my money just to get even. This isn't my fault."

"You wrecked my phone!" I wrench open her blue bag and rummage through. "And you don't even own one."

"Fine." She pulls an El-Q from the table but there's not enough cord to get it close to her face. "But why does it have to be this model?"

"It's way more user friendly. See the big screen and all the icons? These are the apps it comes with." I take the phone from her and open a magazine app just to show her.

"To me, an icon is Alice Munro."

"What songs does she sing? Maybe I can play one for you."

"She writes short stories."

"Oh yeah? You can read on this model, too." I point to a little image of a book. "Here's the icon." Then I click on it. "They've got Charles Dickens on here as a sample. But watch what else this device can do." I tap the centre button and a line appears on the screen along with the words *What can I help you with?*

The line wobbles as I speak. "Find me *A Tale of Two Cities.*"

A female computer voice answers *okay*, and a moment later, the book opens for us.

"It's like having a genie in a cellphone," Susan says.

"That's what they call her. Genie. Great, right?" But as I try to read the opening, the print seems incredibly tiny and the words look blobby. I blink for a few seconds. "Uh, what's wrong with my eyes?"

"Usually, I need glasses to read," Susan tells me. "They're in my purse."

"I'll just bump up the font then." I hit the plus sign a couple of times.

"That is impressive. You would never need reading glasses."

It was the best of times, it was the worst of times, it was the age of wisdom, it was the age of foolishness. I read the lines in my head.

"That's another thing. We don't know each other at all. In order to keep this soul switch a secret, we need to stay in touch. To tell each other stuff."

"You're right. I was a young girl once but things have changed so much. School, too, I bet."

"Aw man, that's in less than two weeks. We'll have our bodies back way before then. Don't you think?"

"I don't know. What do you suppose Eli meant by different endings?"

"Oh, come on, he's just messing with our heads." At least, that's what I hope. I can see where she might hope differently. "Christmas is only five days away. I can't miss that." I shake my head, discouraged, then look around for Van. He seems to be taking his sweet time. "You know what? I'm just going to run out to the kiosk and see about a plan so we can stay in touch with each other. You just play with the El-Q awhile till I get back."

She nods and I hand her the device.

I try to run but forget how bad my knee is. Instead, I hobble, as quickly as I can.

"'Here comes Santa Claus, here comes Santa Claus,'" I sing along to the mall music. At Patches, my favourite boutique, I spot a great sale on jeans, slow down, but then pass the display. I can't try them on in this body.

Then I spot Chael in the distance with Hardeep. My breath freezes, my heart stops. I raise my hand to wave, then quickly put it down again when I see my liver spots. They breeze by and head for an exit, not even a glance my way.

Finally, I arrive at the Telco kiosk. The clerks behind the counter — a tall blond girl and a super-hot guy — chat with each other and don't seem to notice there is a world outside their conversation.

"Excuse me. Excuse me." I feel like I'm begging.

They look away from each other, finally. Their eyes land on me but it's as though they see straight through me. Makes me think about Eli's carnival. I shudder.

Then I cough, *ahem, ahem*, and ask them about phone plans for the El-Q.

The tall blonde takes her time to explain several in detail. My eyes glaze, my brain travels on a little vacation. I watch the super-hot guy look over some paperwork. I wonder if he would like me in my usual body. At some point, over the haze, I hear something about a thirty-day trial share plan where El-Q users get free FaceTime and unlimited calling and texting with each other for sixty dollars a month. Seems perfect for Susan and me.

"Can we get that set up today once we buy our El-Qs?" I ask.

"Sure. And after thirty days, you'll get a discount for using one of their devices, too. We have an agreement with IQ."

I'm just about to tell her that I'll be right back when an alarm sounds. Loud. Painful. I cover my ears and turn away. "What is that?" I ask.

"The IQ store must have caught a shoplifter."

"Really?" Something tells me I better check back in on Susan.

CHAPTER 6

Susan

ALL I WANTED WAS TO USE THIS phone as Alexander Bell originally intended and call my son to let him know I remembered I was coming for supper. But I couldn't even find the numbers on the confounded contraption. I tried to get a sales associate's attention. "Yoo-hoo!" I waved but he rushed by to help someone carry out a large box. "Excuse me!" I called to a young woman with a wide chin. But Mandi (that was the name on her tag) was devoting her attention entirely to typing something into her own contraption.

I even tried summoning that genie in the phone by tapping the middle button. Instantly, the magic words appeared and I thought I was getting somewhere. *What can I help you with?*

I raised my voice so she could hear me. "Call Ron MacMillan!"

A lovely, regretful voice answered, *I'm sorry, you have no contacts listed.*

"Can't you look it up?" No answer. The genie ignored me. Bah! Finally, I just pulled out the cord to walk to one of the lab coats. Instantly, a saxophone blared, loud and louder.

I covered my ears and headed for the door, away from the awful racket. Where was Hallie? Hallie would understand how this machine operated. I stepped out the door to peak my head around and look for her.

Now, I'm surrounded by lab coats. It seems as though I've drawn the attention of all the mad scientists in the store. At last, I'll get some help!

"Don't move," says the same young man who ignored me before. Matt, as his name tag reads, shuffles as if to block my getaway.

"This is a misunderstanding," I begin explaining. "Van is supposed to be helping me but he disappeared."

"Van has been let go," Matt answers.

Hard to look this young man in the eyes; they shift and swirl behind his thick glasses. "In the middle of serving a customer, um, Matt? No wonder he was taking so long."

"Call security," he tells Mandi, who seems to have finally torn her attention away from her own screen.

"Sure thing, Matt." Who knew Mandi had such energy and eagerness in her. With her wide, hard jaw, she looks to be one tough cookie.

The horn continues to blare. Everyone stares in my direction. Nothing like this has ever happened to me in my entire life. It would be rather exciting, if I could just be a bystander watching it happen to someone else.

Mandi frowns at me, pushing that hard chin forward. She could be a boxer or a security guard herself.

She taps something into her contraption. "They'll be here in a moment."

"You don't need security," I tell them. "I'm buying the El-Q. Two of them."

"Sure you are," Mandi says. "Show us the money, kid."

"I don't have it — Hallie, um —" I think quickly about how to explain our relationship in a logical way. The truth would be too unbelievable. "I mean, my grandmother does. She just stepped away. I was looking for her when you stopped me."

"You can't leave the store without paying for the device."

"I understand that. I wasn't leaving completely. Just stepping over the line, as it were. But while we're waiting, maybe you can show me how you make a phone call from this."

Not one of the young people standing around me answers. Instead, like attendants at an insane asylum, they tighten their circle around me.

Meanwhile, two men in black uniforms arrive. Their uniforms have pockets everywhere, even on the legs of their pants. It gives them a bulky, muscular look. What can they possibly need all those pockets for? They can't carry weapons or ammunition in them, surely. But their faces look so stern and serious, I don't ask.

"Would you come this way, miss?"

"But I can't leave the store. My grandmother won't know where I am." The lie comes out a second time, much quicker. I'm getting used to the idea and rather liking it. More fun to have a granny than to be one.

The two men hook their arms under my shoulders, and even though I try to dig my heels in, it's impossible on tile floor. I feel like I'm being abducted. And then finally I see the tall, thin blond woman that used to be me making her way back to the store.

"Grandma, help!" I yell.

"Let her go!" Hallie shouts at the guards. "Immediately," she adds.

The guards look from Hallie to me. You can see the disbelief on their faces. One set of eyebrows rises, another set of eyes narrows in response. What is *wrong* with these people? So our skin colours don't exactly match. This is the twenty-first century.

"Call Uncle Ron! They think I was stealing the El-Q!" I explain. I turn to the guards with all the pockets. "My uncle is a lawyer."

"Ma'am, your" — Mandi raises her fingers in those air quotation marks I find such an affectation — "'granddaughter' disconnected the El-Q and headed through the door. Claims she wanted to know how to call someone. What does she take us for?"

Hallie rolls her eyes, an odd movement for an octogenarian. "I'm sorry. My granddaughter was raised Amish."

The lab coats squint. They are trying to take that literally but don't look convinced. Do they not understand a joke without an LOL sign?

"Where is the sales guy who was serving us?" Hallie asks.

"Van got sacked," I tell her, wondering if *sacked* is a teen word.

"He was short-changing inventory," Matt adds.

"Look, we want to buy two El-Qs and connect them in a hurry. So I dashed over to Telco to ask about service …"

"And now she's back, as you can see!" I gesture toward Hallie.

One of the security guards shakes his head at the other.

"We'll be leaving," the other one announces.

You have to admire someone who can take charge like that and make the correct decision.

"Call us if you need us." It is not exactly clear who he thinks will need them, the lab coats or Hallie.

I suddenly become fed up with these fools in white. "Get us two of these in their boxes and ring them up. I need to call my uncle immediately."

Matt of the swirly eyes looks towards Hallie.

Hallie nods eagerly. "What she said."

He exchanges another look with the strong-chinned Mandi, waves his hand, and she heads for the back.

"She'll meet you at the cash," he tells us.

"Unless someone fires her while we wait." I secretly hope the tough girl does lose her job.

"Listen, ma'am," he says to Hallie, "we're all a bit jumpy since we found out about Van. We don't know how he was moving the stock out. You could have been working with him."

"Well, Matt, now that you know we are your valued customers, how can you make this purchase more pleasant for us?" Hallie smiles a thin-lipped smile as she repeats the inane message that even now flashes across the wall at the back. I'm finding I enjoy her gift for sarcasm.

"Did you wish to purchase an extended warranty today, ma'am?" Matt asks her.

"I think guarantees should come included," I answer instead. They always used to be, I think. The fact that the stores make such a business of selling extended ones always makes me suspicious.

"Smart kid," Matt answers. "The guarantee comes with IQ coaching for a year."

"Really," I say. Hallie looks at me, not saying anything. The strong-chinned girl comes back with the two boxes.

"Listen, Mandi. Ring up the El-Qs with an extended warranty." He sighs. "No extra charge."

"Can we do that?" She squints suspiciously at Matt.

"I'll sign off on it," Matt snaps at her.

"Thank you." I smile at them.

"You're welcome, miss."

Matt smiles, but the smile doesn't quite reach his eyes as he glares at Mandi, who is madly typing.

She hands him her device and he scrawls an initial over the screen with his forefinger. "And how will you be paying for that?"

"Visa," I answer. The two lab coats give me a quizzical look. "Right, Grandma?" I quickly add.

"Yes, quite right." Hallie hunts through my purse for a wallet, and when she opens it, I snatch for the credit card.

"Let me do it, Grandma. I know the code." I grin and then whisper to Hallie, "Watch me so you learn it!" This is the one aspect of technology that I have conquered.

Once the transaction is approved, we leave with our El-Qs in a large golden bag. The rectangular phone boxes inside the bag have the appearance of gold bars. The couple at the Telco store seem to be madly flirting, but they stop as Hallie and I load the gold onto the counter.

"The thirty-day all-you-can text, talk, and surf plan please," Hallie says.

I just smile and nod. We shouldn't need a longer term.

Activating the El-Qs takes forever — a phone call and a review of the features plus a signature on a contract and then another credit card swipe. Hallie is quick to punch in the code even with her knobbly old-lady fingers. Like me, she seems a master shopper. Finally, she drags me down the hall to Perspectives for lunch.

"I'm starving. Aren't you? And I can eat anything I want — just look how skinny I am."

Despite my new young body and sharp brain, I suddenly feel exhaustion setting in. "I don't know about eating, but I could really use a coffee."

CHAPTER 7

Hallie

KNEES ON FIRE AS I LIMP ALONG beside Susan, I'm still pretty happy with my new El-Q and hyped to be going someplace where I don't have to order over a counter. If there's one good thing about being trapped in an old-lady body, it's the power of the credit card that comes with it. The restaurant isn't far. We turn a corner and warm, spicy smells make my stomach growl.

After the flash of the IQ store, Perspectives feels calm and soothing. One Christmas tree near the front twinkles with tiny blue lights, but other than that, it's almost too dark. I yawn. I could use a nap.

An Asian woman with hair to her waist shows us to a booth at the back. Then she hands us each a different menu. Drool forms in my mouth, I'm so hungry; and I'm thin now, so I'm going to order the works! My fingers tremble as I open the cover of the menu, which is just one page. It reminds me of the children's menus you're supposed to order from only until you're eleven. Because I'm short, my parents passed me off as a child right until last year.

The seniors' menu.

I blink a few times and then squint. My menu only lists a few items — is this all I get to choose from? — and I can't even make them out, the print's too small.

"You probably need those reading glasses in my purse." Susan holds a Bible-thick brown menu in front of her, flips the pages forward and then back again. "My, my. The Yuletide special. Prime rib roast beef. I haven't had one of those since my last root canal six years ago." She grins with my lovely teeth and shows my great dimples.

Her eyes are bright green with long, dark eyelashes. Those were mine once; I inherited them from my mom. Would they ever be mine again? A bubble of sick reaches my throat but I swallow it back down. I slam my hand down. *Ow*, that hurt. I just *have* to get back to my body again. I reach into her purse and take a pair of horn-rimmed glasses from a leather case. With them on, I still need to use the flashlight app on my new phone to light the menu.

Susan shakes her head. "I can't believe you bought those things after they nearly had me arrested. We should have just walked away."

"See how useful they are already?" I aim the light on her menu. "Most sales people eyeball teens as if they have sticky fingers. And girls with your skin colour? Well forget about it. You're just not used to it. And, just so you know, my eyes" — I point to hers — "see 20/20." Peering down through the horn rims, I read my choices: turkey, ham, or salmon, all complete with soup, salad, coffee, and dessert.

"You should vote with your dollar! Buy from some-one who treats you properly." She flips a menu page again. "Can I chew beef with your teeth?"

"Yeah. Cavity free on my last checkup." But now the question dawns on me, what can the teeth in my current mouth handle? The soft proteins on my menu may be especially designed for weaker, old teeth. "These El-Qs are the best." I light up the dessert selection with the device in my hand now. "But if I knew we had all the time in the world, I would have walked away from that store, too." Jell-O, rice pudding, or ice cream — not very exciting.

"Death by Chocolate, yum. Your digestion fine with that? I can't believe how hungry I am. It must be this teenaged body."

"We're trying to watch my weight. Don't you dare gain me ten pounds while you're in my body."

"This body is perfect. Why would you need to watch your weight?"

"Because I want a boyfriend. My friend Abby has already had three and she's a toothpick. And if I'm thinner, maybe I'll look taller. Optical illusion, you know? Guys will notice me." I practise a Susan move, pursing my old-lady mouth. I'm going to have to perfect that if I want people to really believe I'm her. Look at those round, healthy cheeks on her. Why didn't I appreciate them when they were mine? "I like this guy named Chael. He calls me thunder thighs. I think he's joking, he's always teasing. Still. Hey, maybe you should take notes on your new phone."

"Or I could do it on the notepaper that's in my purse."

"Okay, but my friends will wonder about you."

She sighs and takes out her El-Q. "Show me."

I insert my old cell's memory card. "Now you have all my contact information." I open the contacts list to show her. "Too bad we can't do that with our brains." I hand the phone back to her and set the preferences on mine to my favourite sound, the burp.

"Where is the boy you like? The one named after the greens." She looks over the names.

"It's actually spelled C-h-a-e-l."

She smiles. "I like the spelling."

"Cool, right?" I open the notepad and virtual key-board. "So, you know my best friend's name is Abby, then there's Megan. She texts me a lot about Chael ... I have a little sister named Aria. My dad has red hair. Obviously, I look more like my mother. My last name is Prince ... are you making notes?"

"So, I just type this information on these flashlight letters on the table here?" She tries it out and squeals as she types. Then she pauses and frowns. "How am I ever going to keep all this straight?"

I shrug my shoulders. "Let's get the El-Q Hangout app. That may help." I take hers and download the pro-gram. While the tiny bar fills to show the progress of the download, I keep thinking out loud. "We need to stay together whenever possible so we can help each other. But everyone will wonder about that ... unless ..."

"Unless what?"

"You did it already back in the IQ store — adopted me as your grandmother. My school has a program something like that to develop empathy. Usually a mom and baby come in. But I don't see why it can't be with a senior. I can earn the forty volunteer hours I need to graduate spending time and helping you. It can be with technology, too, so perfect purchase."

"Only I am currently in your teenaged body and certainly know nothing about El-Qs and such."

"A bit of a hiccup, I admit. But we'll make it work; we have to." The progress bar fills completely now. I open the program and create our profile. "Here you go."

"What did you say your last name was?"

"Prince."

Her fingers beat a rhythm on the virtual keyboard displayed against the tablecloth.

"You're really speedy on that."

"I used to be a court stenographer. You know, I already have grandchildren. I really don't need any more.

"Are they helpful?" I ask.

She shakes her head. "Not at all. They live too far away. It's as though they don't even exist. Aria is your sister," she repeats as she table-types. "The love of your life is Chael. Friends are Abby. And Megan. There now. How do I get books on this thing?"

I show her how to connect with the library on the internet, and using my library card number, we get her Alice Munro's short stories. She grins as though I've given her the best gift ever. Then we open a Facebook account under her name. "I'll have to become friends with your family so I can get to know them," I tell her.

"Friends? But they'll know you as a relative."

"Just a word. Brothers and sisters can be friends on Facebook." She's so amazed with everything that we forget about ordering. Neither of us realizes the waitress is standing there till she coughs.

"Do you need another moment?" Her voice sounds annoyed.

"No, no!" I answer. "I'll have the soup, turkey, and the ice cream for dessert."

"Ginger pumpkin or curried lentil, ma'am?" the waitress asks.

"Take the pumpkin," Susan says. "You know the lentil doesn't agree with you."

Yuck! "I've changed my mind. I'll have the salad, instead. Ranch dressing, please."

The waitress nods as she writes. Then she looks up at Susan.

"I'll have the Yuletide special with the Yorkshire pudding, a baked potato, and all the works, sour cream, butter, bacon. A Caesar salad, extra bacon there, too. Dessert's not included with mine?"

"No, miss."

"Well, I want to die by chocolate anyway."

"Very well. How do you like your beef?"

"Rare. Very rare."

"Good. Your salads will be coming up shortly." She takes our menus.

Meanwhile I show Susan her son's Facebook page.

"Oh, look at that lovely picture of Ron Junior playing soccer!" she says. "He rarely has time for that anymore. So busy with work."

"Junior? He's like forty-something." Who knew forty-year-olds even played soccer.

"His father, my ex, is Ron Senior." She shudders for a moment. "Can we look at my daughter's page? She lives on the Coast."

"Doesn't matter where anybody lives. If she's on Facebook, sure. What's her name?"

"Emily MacMillan. MacMillan's my last name. Emily doesn't use her married name. She's very modern."

Once I find Emily, Susan's even more excited. "That's my granddaughter, Leah!" She points out a little girl in a photo. "And she's wearing the top I sent her for her birthday. I didn't know she liked it. She never sent me a thank-you note!"

I shrug. "Bet she would text you, if you give her your number. Let's message your daughter."

Susan finishes typing a long message as our salads arrive. Our waitress plunks a dish right on the virtual keyboard and the letters glow from the Caesar salad.

"What is with her?" I say as I crunch into my salad.

"How do I finish?" Susan's still caught up in her letter.

"Move the salad. Just so you know, normally Facebook messages are only a couple of lines."

"Really?"

"Yes! You should eat now," I say loudly so she focuses on something else besides her phone.

"Oh, right, certainly! How do I send my letter?" Susan asks.

"Press enter."

She smiles at the screen, then finally sets it aside and

rubs her hands. "Yum!" she says as she bites into her first mouthful of romaine. Our main dishes arrive and she immediately saws off a piece of beef. "Oh, this is so good. How's yours?"

"Blah." The turkey is mushy. Maybe they cook it that way so old folks don't choke. The fries are as pale as my skin.

The waitress comes back to ask how everything is and that's when I see it. The tattoo above her knuckles. *Carpe Diem*. "Eli? You're a girl now?"

"Shhh!" Finger to her lips, she looks around to see if anyone has overheard. "I don't want to be defined by any one sex."

"What are you doing here?" Susan whispers.

"Contrary to popular belief, I like to be everywhere," Eli answers. "Just want to see how you two are getting on."

"Famously," Susan says.

"Horribly," I say at exactly the same time. There's an awkward pause when Eli and Susan look from each other to me and back again. "Okay, I didn't exactly mean we weren't getting along. It's not that at all, it's about this, this wrinkly old skin." I point a finger down my throat in a gag-me gesture.

More awkward silence.

"Come on, Eli. Just how long am I stuck in this body?"

CHAPTER 8

Susan

I STARE AT ELI IN HIS NEW long-haired-waitress format and wonder almost the same thing as Hallie does. *How much longer can I possibly have in this body?* But for me, I ask myself that same question each and every morning when I get up — right after, *Am I still alive?*

Today, it's not a complaint. I'm happy in this smooth, unwrinkled, young body. Today, I want life to continue forever. Nothing aches, everything works, eyes, ears, teeth, even my voice. Whereas poor Hallie sounds desperate to be her young self again, and I can't blame her. Hallie must hate my old snakeskin as much as I do.

"If you like, we can head back to the carnival, celebrate Christmas there. You can both ride the roller coaster," Eli suggests, smiling. He's really a very becoming woman. Golden specks float in his now-brown eyes. His long, black hair lies smooth and glossy down his back.

Still, why must he taunt the teen so?

"I want my real life back. The ordinary one," Hallie complains, running her fingers through her blond hair. (I refuse to let my hair go grey, even if I grow to be a hundred.) It gets stuck halfway. After all, Hallie is used to a short pixie hairdo; fingers would have been the perfect comb. But not with her current fine, long hair.

"Everyone lives their life for a reason, a purpose. And the goal can't just be kissing a boy." Eli still smiles but his brown eyes flash bright like sharpened knives.

"But I don't know what I want to be when I grow up," Hallie whines. "I have a hard enough time choosing what to wear in the morning."

"Because everything's all about you!" Eli sighs. "You haven't looked outside yourself to find what the world wants from you yet. This body transposition should help."

"Yes, but how long will it take?" She huffs.

His eyes squint, his chin lifts. Can she not see she's making him angry? Probably not. What is that expression? *You can't put an old head on a young body.* This transposition creates the worst possible opposite effect: a young brain in an old body.

"Christmas is in five days. Can I have my body back by then? *Pu-lease*?"

"Time!" Eli waves a long slender hand as though dismissing the concept. "You want everything instantly. Even texting doesn't happen so quickly."

"That's it, isn't it? All this is because you hate technology."

"No. Just the amount of time you spend on it. And you've hooked Susan on it, too, now I see."

He's caught me glancing toward the screen — I thought I heard some music — the ringtone? If only I'd known how much fun these things were a long time ago.

Ron kept trying to talk me into buying a computer but I thought it would take up too much room in my condo. Besides, I have a telephone. Why do I need to communicate via keyboard and screen? I did enough keyboarding in the courtrooms to support the family. I didn't want to do it in my spare time. This unit, however, is like a small pocket book, the perfect size.

The El-Q plays that music again and I turn to Eli. "May I take this? It could be a message from my daughter, Emily."

"Who cares!" Eli waves a hand again. "You two haven't discussed the car problem and how to fix it. Direct your energies that way."

"Is that my goal?" Hallie sputters. "To prove an eighty-two-year-old can still drive?"

"Free will! So much work, isn't it?" Eli says. "You decide the real direction of your life. Or the direction of your death. But I'm going to help you out on that time thing, since you're so impatient. You've got till Christmas Eve. Then I take over. Now enjoy the rest of the meal while I get your desserts." His long hair barely ripples as he turns away and heads back for the kitchen.

Hallie's brow furrows, her eyes narrow. She purses her thin blue lips. She's getting good at that.

I pick up the El-Q. "It's Abby." I read out loud from the screen. *Are you okay? Are you still with the old biddy?* I raise an eyebrow at Hallie and smile. She's the old biddy now. How does that feel? Then I read out loud as I type back: "Actually, yes. She's quite nice. She bought me a really expensive phone and a nice lunch."

"Don't press send. That's not the way I talk. Here." Hallie snatches the El-Q and types. *Everything's cool. Got the El-Q :-) Eating lunch. See you.* She shows me, then her thumb hits send. "My friends text a lot ... I don't know how this is going to work." She frowns.

"I can write shorter. In the old days, it cost money to use an envelope and stamp. We had to make it count."

Hallie stares down at the El-Q. "I just wish I could talk to Abby myself."

"One way or another, this will only be for a few days. That's how Eli made it sound." I smile at the "old biddy" and pat her gnarled, wrinkly hand with my smooth, soft one.

Her eyes fill.

"I'm sorry."

"Yeah, well, you should be." Hallie pulls her hand from under mine. "This is all your fault."

I sigh. I can see why she annoys Eli. "You've made up your mind about me." I shake my head at her. "But I've been driving since I was your age."

"And your reflexes suck. You didn't hit the brake fast enough, or we wouldn't be here."

"Oh yes I did!" I slam my hands on the table. "The gas pedal locked."

"Well, *excuse me* if I don't want to believe something till I see it for myself."

It's no use losing my temper at her. I take another deep breath and lower my voice again. "That's fine. You heard Eli. You need to find your own goal. In the meantime, just to let you know, with your new pale colouring and dry skin, it helps to keep applying lipstick. Otherwise your lips disappear."

At that moment, Eli swoops in front of me and sets down a gigantic dish full of melted and solid chunks of chocolate topped with white clouds of whipped cream. "Mmm. Lovely. Thank you!" I tell him.

He sets a small parfait glass full of pink ice cream in front of Hallie. She groans.

"Will there be anything else for you ladies today?" Eli waits, grinning, hands curled into his hips.

"Just the bill," Hallie says and stabs into her strawberry ice cream.

I savour my first mouthful. Warm and sweet, fluffy and smooth, all the textures and tastes of heaven in a dessert called Death.

Hallie shovels her ice cream into her mouth.

"You know, you didn't have to order off the seniors' menu. That was just Eli's little joke on you."

"Now you tell me!"

"Yes, well it's cheaper this way. I don't want you spending all my retirement money."

Hallie continues to stab at the pink melting lump and then spoons it in. "Ow, ow, ow!" Hallie's hands suddenly shoot up to her jaws. "You can't even eat ice cream with these teeth!" she shrieks.

"Of course you can," I explain. "Only slowly. You mustn't let the cold part hit your molars. Keep the ice cream on your tongue instead and let it melt there."

Eli swoops around again, this time with the bill. "Everything okay, ladies?" he asks brightly.

"Perfect," I tell him as Hallie glowers. It's remarkable to me that an eighty-two-year-old face can look so much like that of a sullen teen's. What can I do to try to cheer her up? It's been so long since I was actually a young person myself, it's hard to think. I do remember looking forward to getting freedom and independence, especially my driver's licence, the very thing I'm most reluctant to give up now. I pat Hallie's hand again. "Pay the bill, dear."

Hallie slaps down my Visa like it's the winning card at a poker game. A poker game that she may, in fact, be losing.

"You know, I was a single mom. My whole life I scrimped and saved so my kids could have the best," I tell Hallie, hoping it will make her more conservative in her future spending.

"Don't worry," Hallie answers when Eli returns with the credit card machine. "I'm not going to leave the waitress any tip."

Eli rolls his eyes as he tears the receipt from the machine and hands it back. "Have a nice day."

"You, too!" Hallie says.

From the table we head to the washroom and I watch as Hallie finds my brightest lipstick and applies it.

"Allow me." I remove a small brush from our blue purse and arrange Hallie's pale blond hair to its greatest volume. Hallie, in turn, sticks her fingers through my hair expertly, fingering a few sections into curls.

"May I?" I ask and then borrow back my own bright red lipstick. "This body comes with such luscious lips."

"Hmm. That's a nice look." Hallie nods.

"Good, something I've taught you then." I turn to her and touch her shoulder. "Listen, it's only four days to Christmas Eve. I'm sure you'll get your body back by then. And in the meantime, you get to drive the Hurricane and take us home."

CHAPTER 9

Hallie

THE HURRICANE FEELS NOTHING like my Uncle Bill's truck, which rides rumbly and rough. Instead of smelling like hay and manure, there's a vinyl, gluey, new-car aroma to it. I love it. I turn the key, glide the transmission into drive, and off we go. Hey, Abby, look at me go! But then I notice my knobby knuckles on the steering wheel, the bulgy blue veins and brown spots on my hands. Scratch that, better she doesn't see.

Still, I'm a great driver and the engine runs smooth, like it's not even on. Violins play some classical version of "Good King Wenceslas," a great soundtrack to my drive, relaxing me. When I take my foot off the gas pedal, the Hurricane instantly slows down. So much for Susan's stupid excuse for backing up over me.

We stop at the intersection leading out of the mall parking lot. Snowbanks line the road but they're turning slushy in the afternoon sun.

"Hey, over there." I point for Susan's sake. "That's Chael and Hardeep walking! Smile, you know them. Wave back!"

"Which one is which?" Susan asks.

"The one smiling is Chael. He's the guy I like. The short guy with the Union Jack cap, that's Hardeep."

"Oh, my, but his eyes are interesting. Who's that girl walking away from them?" She points to Kendra, who has miles of legs and smooth, dark brown hair. Chael grins.

"Just some fungus from school. Kendra's all over Chael."

"He seems to like her."

A car honks behind us. I roll my eyes. "Which way?" I ask.

"Turn left. Follow Guelph Road."

Sunlight sparkles off the melting snow so that I have to squint when I check for other cars. As I turn my head, my neck cricks. I turn the other way, and it cricks again. *Ow!* I flip the indicator.

All clear.

The driver behind us leans on the horn.

"Oh, hold your horses!" Susan yells as we slowly inch out onto Guelph and approach the overpass. The light turns red.

"Where to?" I ask.

"We need to go back to the Saji dealership. They should look at the gas pedal."

"Right." My eyes roll — I can't even help it — and I sigh. "Is that anywhere close?"

"Ten-minute ride on the expressway. "

"What? I drive dirt roads on farms. I've never been on an expressway before."

"Better than navigating all the streets and stoplights. Should be easier than driving a truck on a farm road." She pats my shoulder. "You'll do fine."

"And what am I going to tell the mechanics?" I ask. "That I backed up over you?"

"Tell them they haven't fixed the problem. By the way, you're going to dinner at my son Ron's tonight. He and his wife, Sheryl, want to talk about Sunnyside Terrace." She grins at me. "Trust me, driving the expressway and visiting the garage will be more fun."

"What is Sunnyside? Some kind of home?"

"A retirement residence with full-time nurses. They think you need that now."

"You have to come with!" I tell her.

"Why? You'll do better without me. Just agree with everything they say."

"Good, I'll sign you up."

"You assume it will be me who ends up at Sunnyside. What if Eli decides it will be you?"

I shudder. "That won't happen, will it? Do you honestly think Eli would do that to me?"

"I don't know." Susan raises her eyebrows. "He only said he'd make something happen by Christmas Eve. He didn't say what." She nods to the intersection. "Green light."

I ease the Hurricane forward.

Susan points to the entrance ramp. "Over there!"

"All right, expressway, here I come." I grip the steering wheel so tight my knuckles grow knobbier.

"You'll like it. Go, go! You can't just stop, there are cars behind us."

Gently, I push down on the gas pedal and steer onto the ramp, veer around the curves till I get on the highway.

"Faster. You'll cause an accident. Most people drive at least the speed limit."

I press down harder. A sign at the side of the road posts that limit at 100 kilometres per hour. The road looks dry and clear but I've never driven that fast. The needle on the speedometer hits 70. *Ahhh!* What a rush. I smile.

"You enjoy driving, don't you?"

"What's not to like? I'm in control of a new car."

I throw a glance into the side mirror. A minivan with a large dog hanging out the side passes us. Then a school bus full of kids. Suddenly, a horn honks loud and long. An eighteen-wheel truck barrels past and the Hurricane shudders from its wind.

"Maybe just a little faster," Susan suggests.

I push the pedal harder and the Hurricane surges forward. The needle on the speedometer leans forward to the 100 mark. I can do this. Just keep the wheel steady and press that gas. Like Susan says, it's way easier than driving an old truck on a bumpy dirt road. I shiver as I watch the needle lean toward 110.

"The police often set up just past that overpass. I know I told you to drive faster, but now slow down for this next bit."

I ease my foot up but nothing much happens. Instead, the Hurricane surges ahead.

Susan grabs my arm. "You need to slow down!"

I switch my foot to the brake and press down. Nothing happens. My stomach lurches. So much for control. The needle hits 120, passes it, and leans into 130. I pump the brake now.

"Hallie!"

"I can't stop!" The needle points at 140. I steer like mad around the eighteen-wheeler, then drive around the minivan in the centre lane. We fly into the passing lane. Ahead, the school bus chugs along.

"Why is it in the passing lane?" I hit the horn and some little kids wave at us from the back of the bus.

In the passenger mirror, I spot the minivan catching up to us in the centre lane.

I can feel adrenalin snapping through my chest and brain. My heart actually hurts. Instead of braking, I slam my foot back on the accelerator and steer hard to the right. We cut ahead of the minivan, which also steers right to get out of our way. The driver leans on his horn.

"Nicely done," Susan says.

From somewhere behind, a siren warbles. Oh perfect!

She shrugs. "Don't worry. Just hit the brake again and keep your foot there."

I stomp down on the left pedal and Susan pulls the gear leaver into neutral. "See if you can steer to the shoulder."

I pull the wheel to the right, forcing the Hurricane to cut in front of the minivan a second time. The driver waves his fist at me. Too bad. We have bigger problems.

In the mirror I spot the squad car, tiny like a toy car. Not like he can help us at all. I have to figure how to get out of this myself.

I swing hard to the right and steer onto the shoulder. It's plenty wide enough for a car. We crunch along the icy snow. Safe.

Susan reaches over and turns the key, switching the ignition off. "That should do it."

Only it doesn't. The Hurricane continues.

My blood runs cold when I spot him — a man on a motorcycle in our path up ahead. Seriously, in the winter? He's wearing a red leather jacket with furry white cuffs and he has a white beard. "Oh my God! It's Santa on a Harley."

"Why doesn't he just go!" Susan yanks up the emergency brake.

He kicks off his stand and balances on his seat, fiddling with something on his boot.

We're starting to slow down now. The speedometer clocks us at 60 now. But we'll still never stop in time. I swing the steering wheel to the left. "It's not turning!" I scream.

"Power steering! It won't work now that I've shut the engine." She hits the horn and waves frantically at him.

The motorcyclist doesn't even look back at us. Still picking at his boot.

Fifty kilometres, 40. We're going to kill Santa.

I lean on the horn, and Susan and I both scream at him. "Move!"

Finally, he turns to us and his mouth drops. He guns it.

The Hurricane hits the side of his saddlebag. The motorcycle wobbles but manages to pull away.

The Hurricane drives on but the speedometer needle now drops steadily: 30 … 20 … 10.

The siren grows louder. The squad looms larger in the mirror and then pulls in behind us as we roll to a stop.

The police officer gets out and approaches slowly.

"Oh great!" I bury my head in my arms.

"Stay calm."

A heavyset blond woman with a tight French braid tucked under the back of her Cossack cap squints at the car from different angles.

Susan nudges me. "Roll down your window."

I hit the button over and over. "It's not working!"

"Right, the engine's off." Susan sighs. "Just open the door."

I fumble for the handle and finally get it open. A blast of cold air hits me.

"Good afternoon, ma'am. My name is Officer Meryl Wilson. How are you this afternoon?" Her mirrored sunglasses reflect back my wrinkled-apple-doll face.

I gasp, shocked again by the pale skin and wrinkles.

Officer Wilson's brow furrows. "Are you feeling all right?" She sticks her head in so close to mine I can smell her cinnamon gum. She pauses and sniffs at me.

What, do I smell like old lady, too? "I'm fine. It's just that —"

She cuts me off. "Have you been taking any meds today?"

"Grandma takes baby aspirin for her heart. Nitroglycerine when she has an episode. Blood pressure medication. Nothing else," Susan answers for me.

Maybe I should pop a nitro around now.

One eyebrow raises above those sunglasses. "May I see your licence, registration, and insurance, please?"

Susan opens the glove compartment and hands me some papers, which I pass to her. "The licence is in your wallet," she says quietly.

"Is there any reason your granddaughter is helping you so much today?" Officer Wilson's eyes shift constantly, checking out the back of the car, my passenger, and then back to my face. "Are you feeling confused?"

Oh, you have no idea, I think. Out loud, I scramble to lie. "No, no. Nervous is all." I fumble with cold, stiff fingers through Susan's wallet, find the licence, and pass it to Officer Wilson.

"So tell me, were you having an episode back there?" she asks.

"No. Really, I'm fine."

"Anything to drink this afternoon?" she asks.

"Just a coffee and a glass of water," I answer. "Oh, you mean like alcohol? No, nothing."

"You were driving erratically. Any idea how fast you were going?"

"I can explain."

"Save it." The officer walks back to her car and I shut the door to keep in some warmth.

"She's running your plate and licence," Susan explains.

"Get a lot of tickets, do you?" I snap.

"No. I watch *LA Cops*."

In the rear-view mirror, I can see the officer probably doing exactly what Susan said. Her head seems down a long time. I see a clipboard. Finally, she returns. I open the door again and she hands me back Susan's papers and licence, as well as a ticket.

"I'm going easy on you. You were driving 40 kilometres over the speed limit — weaving in and out of traffic …"

"Officer, honestly, I had to …"

Susan touches my arm and shakes her head.

"But I'm lowering your speed by 10 kilometres and only giving you a ticket for speeding. You'll get demerit points but nothing like if I charged you with stunt driving."

Stunt driving at eighty-two? "But my accelerator stuck. I've had the car in the garage for the problem. In fact, we're just going back to the Saji dealership now to have the mechanic look at it again."

"Really? Well, in that case, ma'am, I don't feel this vehicle is safe. I'm going to have to impound it."

Susan elbows me hard now and points to the dealership, which is just off the next exit. So close we could walk.

"Officer, please, we would like our mechanic to deal with this problem. He looked at it this morning and he's just over there. The Saji tow truck could be here in seconds."

She looks up to where Susan is pointing and frowns. "All right. Go ahead and call him. I'll just stay in the car and wait."

CHAPTER 10

Susan

WHILE IDLING IS AGAINST THE law for the rest of Halton, the police officer stays nice and warm in her squad car, engine running. Meanwhile, she makes Hallie and I sit in the cold Hurricane. Hallie's teeth are chattering and I offer her my ski jacket.

She refuses it. Proud little thing, I like that about her. She reminds me of me in more ways than just the body.

Thankfully, the tow truck arrives quickly, before she freezes to her pride.

"So we lose the car and get a ticket?" Hallie complains as she struggles out of the Hurricane.

"No. We'll fight the ticket in court once the Saji mechanic fixes it and writes up the bill."

The tow truck driver is a burly man with long hair flowing from under his Blue Jays cap, and thick fingers that constantly adjust it. "This is a new car and it won't start? Do you want me to try?"

"She is not to drive it anymore." The officer joins us now. "It is an unsafe vehicle."

"Oh, *ohhh*!" the driver answers, as though there is a

secret message being conveyed between them: the client is a confused old lady who is dangerous behind the wheel. He busies himself, hitching the Hurricane to his truck, raising the front half off the ground.

"Do you want a lift home?" Officer Wilson asks.

"No, we want to go to the garage and talk to the mechanic," Hallie answers.

"All right. Have a good day. Drive safely," the officer calls to the tow truck driver, who waves back.

When he's satisfied the Hurricane is secure, the driver opens the door on the passenger side and I grab Hallie's elbow to help her up into the truck.

She shrugs me off the moment she's seated. I don't blame her. It's what I do, too, when I'm saddled with that creaking old body. Refuse help, act crotchety when it's forced on me. I slide in beside Hallie.

"Looks like the snow's all going to melt this afternoon," the driver prattles cheerily as he starts up his truck. "You have all your Christmas shopping done?"

"No!" Hallie answers in the one curt word.

Her old body has to be weary to the bone so I try to cover for her rudeness by changing the subject. "It's so warm out someone was riding their motorcycle!"

"Diehards!" The driver shakes his head.

"He nearly died hard. We hit him when the accelerator stuck," Hallie grumbles.

"Did the gas pedal really stick down? 'Cause it's the electronic throttle plate opening that causes a car to speed up."

"I don't know," Hallie answers.

He's raised an interesting point. I try to remember the sensation of my foot against the accelerator but, of course, whenever the Hurricane sped out of control, I quickly switched and stomped the brake. Who knows whether the gas pedal actually stayed down or not.

"I towed a guy the other day who swore his car's computer went crazy when he couldn't slow his car down. Your gas pedal just sends a signal to the car's computer to open that throttle plate."

"What kind of car?" I ask. "Do you have his name?"

"Um … I can't remember. Just that he didn't want to drive his either."

Does he really not remember? Or does he need to keep the other owner's information secret for some reason, a privacy act or an agreement with Saji Motors. I raise an eyebrow and nod to Hallie to signal her.

If we can find someone else who has the same problem, say a man, not too young but not too old, either — someone willing to testify for us — maybe the judge will believe him when we fight our speeding ticket.

I help Hallie out at the service entrance and the driver tows the Hurricane through the open garage door. There are three podium desks in the large car hangar, each decorated with a little bit of artificial evergreen and a big red bow. Season's Greetings to us all as we charge you an enormous fat bill for fixing your vehicle.

I point to the farthest podium. "That's the man who served me last time." The technician standing there is tall and bald with shaggy white eyebrows.

"Mr. Clean?" Hallie asks.

I nod. Not quite the fellow on the cleaner bottle, but almost.

As we stroll up to him, he grips the top of the podium like a preacher about to deliver a sermon. "Well, good afternoon, Susan, back so soon? How are you?"

"Fine, thanks, James, how are you?" Hallie answers, addressing the technician by the name on his tag.

Neither really cares how the other one actually feels, it's all just condescending politeness, if you ask me. Like James addressing an eighty-two-year-old by her first name, and Hallie addressing him the same way.

Of course, service people never give out surnames in case customers try to track them down after work hours. Makes every transaction start on too personal a note. If you're kind and friendly to the old fool, she'll go away and stop bothering you.

"We were on the highway, my granddaughter and I, when the accelerator stuck," Hallie explains.

I like that she continues to refer to me as her granddaughter; it makes me more comfortable with our odd attachment. I feel closer to her than to my own grandkids; we're almost like two halves of the same soul rather than just two bodies with each other's souls.

"The gas pedal gave you problems again?" the technician says. "I thought we tacked that mat down nicely." He steps away from his tall desk and scrutinizes her shoes. "And you're wearing proper footwear."

"Same as this morning," Hallie answers.

She's wearing the expensive Zikees I bought when my friend Linda convinced me we could start jogging.

"So that's not it, either. Are you sure you stepped on the brake when you wanted to slow down? You didn't confuse the gas pedal with the brake, did you? It's easy enough to do."

I shake my head, picturing the kind of senile idiot who would stomp on the accelerator over and over to stop an out-of-control vehicle. "My grandma's foot was on the brake. I saw it!" I tell him.

"Did you, by any chance, try hooking your foot under the pedal to unstick it?"

"No," Hallie answers. "I was busy braking — and steering. We nearly creamed a busload of kids on the expressway."

His eyebrows reach for the sky. "All right, then. Well, we'll run another diagnostic on your Hurricane. See if we come up with something else this time. Do you need a lift home?"

"We prefer to wait for the repair," Hallie insists.

"But there are cars ahead of you. You don't have an appointment," James tells her.

"Sure we do. Remember, it was scheduled for this morning. You just extended it to this afternoon by not solving the problem."

James stares at her an extra moment, unblinking.

Good for Hallie. How many people would stand up to this bureaucratic bully, let alone someone under twenty?

"Okay." He lifts his fingers from the desk and drops them helplessly. "You know where the waiting room is. I've got your keys here. We'll call you when it's ready."

We walk out of the garage area into the main building. I lead the way to the chairs and magazines and the single-serve coffee maker. "Do you want me to make you a hot chocolate?" I ask. Hallie probably needs something sweet as well as hot to recover from the shock and cold of that drive and the wait along the highway.

Hallie nods and takes out her El-Q.

"Candy cane, white chocolate, or regular chocolate?" I ask as I read the flavours on the lids.

"Candy cane," Hallie answers.

I choose and arrange a little pod in the machine and place a cup under the spout. The waiting area is just an extension of the showroom, where three of the walls are glass. In one corner, a large artificial tree stands decorated with red bows, gold-sprayed pinecones, and construction paper cars with names written on them. Through that side, we can see the gleaming new Saji models: two subcompacts (an electric blue Tsunami sedan and a black hatchback), their sports car (a fire-engine-red Volcano), a midsize luxury (a champagne-coloured Blizzard), and the SUV (a white Hurricane). All named after natural disasters, which should have been my first warning. I originally wanted the Tsunami hatchback, but my son had insisted I needed the larger Hurricane to keep me protected. As if I were going to play bumper cars with the vehicle and needed the additional armour.

Through the other two glass walls, we can see the outside, watch rush hour traffic stream by as the sun sinks and the sky darkens. A gurgle and hiss signals that the hot chocolate is ready, and I remove the cup and hand it to Hallie. "Should I text your mom about where you are?"

"Yeah. What time is your son expecting you?"

"Five. You're going to get a lecture about keeping track of time and being late."

"Wow. Sounds like you have less freedom than I do."

"Sometimes it feels like I'm their child instead of the other way around." I insert another pod to make a hot chocolate for myself. "So you're going to help with this car issue, are you?"

"Absolutely. I don't understand why no one ever believes you."

"Did *you,* until you experienced it yourself?"

Hallie bunches up her mouth awkwardly.

So many wrinkles around that mouth, I should have used a moisturizer when I was a young woman. "Does anyone ever admit they were speeding just for the heck of it?" I shrug. "Or because they are too decrepit to drive and therefore don't pay attention to the speedometer at all?"

"You knew exactly what to do to bring the Hurricane to a safe stop," Hallie tells me.

"Experience. You're a pretty good driver, too, especially for your age. Calm in a disaster." I take my own hot chocolate to the chair beside Hallie and sit down.

She stares in the direction of the Christmas tree. "I didn't buy anyone's gifts."

"I've already given the children all their cheques. Money is all they ever want. I wish I knew them well enough to give them something more personal. More meaningful."

"My cousins come over on Christmas Eve and we play charades."

"Ron and Sheryl and I go out for brunch." She sighs. "Nice to have family traditions." We both sip now and watch a young woman and man embrace near the tree. There's mistletoe hanging from the ceiling. He moves her underneath and she laughs as he bends over to kiss her.

Hallie sighs.

"You can still shop for your family, you live across from the mall now. And you can use my credit card."

"Will I be able to give the presents to them myself, though?" She holds out her hands, palms up, fingers spread. In question and frustration.

"Hopefully."

The couple pull apart and walk away hand in hand. Another sigh from Hallie.

"But you've never been kissed by a boy. Do you want me to use my experience to get you that boyfriend?"

"*Ew*, you're going to go after Chael? But you're ancient."

"On good days, I still feel like a teenager inside, though."

"Still. It's not like I'm going to feel his lips through you."

"True." My turn to sigh. "But you just have to believe that Eli's going to give your body back by Christmas. Just as soon as you achieve whatever he wants for you."

She shakes her head. "He's always annoyed with me. I can't see him giving me what I want." Hallie drinks her hot chocolate quietly for a bit. Thinking things over, perhaps? Finally, she finishes the beverage, crumples her cup, and tosses it into the bin. "You know what? Sure. See if you can get Chael to really like me. And we'll both just have to hope for the best with this body swap."

CHAPTER 11

Hallie

WHEN MR. CLEAN FINALLY CALLS us to say the Hurricane is ready, he hands me a bill of six-hundred dollars.

Susan leans over and looks at it. "Are you kidding?" She throws open her arms and raises her voice. "The car is still under warranty!"

Mr. Clean squints at the angry teenager, then ignores her and speaks to me. "I had to charge for the computer diagnosis since it's the second one today and the mechanic still didn't find any error codes."

"Well, that shows his incompetence. I don't see that it's something we should pay for," Susan says.

I nudge her with my elbow — she's breaking our cover — but then add, "My granddaughter has a point. We just bought an El-Q for that price. And it has a genie in it."

"My mechanic spent an hour cleaning the electronic throttle plate to make sure no carbon buildup was keeping it open. We also installed a steel reinforcement bar to modify excess friction" — *blah, blah, blah, blah* — "None of these are warranty items."

Whatever. I give him my hardest stare. Would the bill be enough to convince the judge to drop the speeding charge? Hopefully. I'm glad they did something so that I can drive this SUV again — driving being one of the few pluses of growing up, I think.

I pay the cashier using Susan's credit card, the other plus.

"Would you like to donate five dollars to our Coins for Cars Christmas fund?" the perky ponytailed girl asks.

"Sure, add it to my bill."

"Five dollars is not coin," Susan mutters under her breath.

"So? It's good karma," I tell her. "I need it to get my Christmas back."

"Here you go." The cashier gives us two red construction paper cars and a marker. "Do you want to write your names on?"

"Yup." I print Hallie in all caps and Susan writes her name in cursive. The cashier doesn't even look at what we wrote. Could have been "Saji cars kill!"

"I can hang these on the tree for you. Would you like to become a member of our Saji Happy Motoring Club?"

Susan snorts, flaring her nostrils like a horse. She looks like she wants to jump the counter and kick the girl.

"How much will that cost?" I ask.

"It's complimentary. You can book appointments online. Earn valuable bonus points. Enter contests. Chat with other happy customers."

"What about unhappy customers?" Susan grumbles.

"Come again?" the girl asks.

"Maybe later," I answer.

Susan scowls as we make our way to the car and drive off.

"Look, I don't know what you wanted me to do about that bill. Leave the car?"

She snorts again.

"Can you just look for the GPS app and punch in my address, so I know how to drive you home?"

She struggles with the El-Q, and I take her through, step by step, giving her the street and house number. Then I tell her to do the same with my device but to key in her home address and her son's. Keeps her busy and she seems to be getting more comfortable with the phone. "By the way, Mom's on my case about my room. You may want to clean it when you get to my house. And clear the dishes after supper, that's my job."

"Well, you're supposed to be at Ron's by now and Sheryl's a real stickler about time."

I shrug. "What can they do to an adult who's late, ground you?"

Susan doesn't answer, just gives a grumpy look and a shrug.

Finally, we get to my house and stop. Susan springs out.

"Keep the El-Q on and stay in touch!" I call after her. "I can help you through stuff that way."

I watch her as she waits on the porch for a moment, then opens the door. I should rush off now, since I'm so late. But I end up staring at the picture window. The glow from the inside of the house turns the living room window into a giant viewing screen with Susan as the star of the show. She heads down the hall to the bright light of the kitchen. My favourite room of the house. There's Mom. She hugs Susan. I swallow hard. I want to be the star of the show playing at my home. I want that hug.

I wipe my eyes and finally drive off, following the GPS instructions to get to Susan's son's house. "Turn left on Spruce," the clipped British computer-voice says. "Turn right on Poplar." It isn't that far, but still the time on the El-Q reads 5:45 by the time I roll into his driveway. Not that late. Who eats supper at five, anyways?

Ringing the doorbell, I hear a shrill female voice. "Your mother's here, finally! Better get your coat on." I'm guessing it's Sheryl.

Why do they need their coats if I'm coming for dinner? The door opens.

A short woman with dark eyes and long, streaked, golden hair smiles at me as she steps out of the house. The man with her I recognize from Facebook as Ron. He's a tall baby-faced guy with kind blue eyes and very fair skin. He probably gets that from me, or the body genes I'm carrying these days.

"Hi, Mom." Ron kisses my cheek quickly and then tugs me along.

I hate this. Why can't I walk at my own pace?

"Good, you didn't block us," Sheryl says as she jumps in the beige-coloured Blizzard, the luxury midsize Saji.

"What's the rush, where are we going?" I shrug him off once I'm seated in the back.

Ron's cheeks flush pink. "We have an appointment at Sunnyside Terrace."

"The chef is making us dinner." Sheryl looks down at her cellphone. "They're wondering where we are!"

"No one told me we were going there."

"It's a surprise," Sheryl says. "A nice free meal and a quick tour. I'm sure you'll like it. It's such a pretty building."

They've obviously seen it before and want me to like it.

The Blizzard lurches forward and Ron boots it. Pretty sure the speed limit is much lower on this street.

"I had an incident on the QEW."

"What? You didn't have an accident, did you?" Sheryl asks. "Are you okay?" She twists her neck. "Your car looks fine."

"No accident, although it was close. The —"

"I don't know why you don't give up your licence and leave the driving to us," Sheryl interrupts. "Statistics show that a cab would be cheaper than all the gasoline and insurance."

"Why do you drive a car, then?" I ask.

"Well, Ron and I need one for work, obviously."

"I like driving," I say on Susan's behalf, but it's true for me, too. "It makes me feel free. Anyway, the gas pedal stuck again. And a police officer wrote me a speeding ticket."

"But you were supposed to have the accelerator looked at," Sheryl says.

"That's all part of owning a car — looking after it, too," Ron adds, keeping his hands on the steering wheel and looking straight ahead. "You used to tell us that all the time."

"I don't need your lecture," I snap.

Whoa! There's a moment of silence where Sheryl and Ron give each other quick looks.

"I did take the Hurricane in this morning. The technician thought it was a crooked car mat. Turns out he was wrong. I took it back this afternoon, and they installed a reinforcement bar."

"Why would you need one of those? The Hurricane's brand new, for heaven's sake," Ron says. "I swear, they just see a senior coming and they invent things ..."

"The Hurricane sped off on me, even though I had my foot on the brake. No one invented that problem."

Sheryl gives Ron a quick look, and I can see the eye-roll thing happening with the daughter-in-law.

Okay, in my other body, I am the queen of the eye roll. It's my favourite form of self-expression. Now that I'm an old biddy, I don't find it so cute.

"So now Ron's supposed to take off work to fight your speeding ticket ..."

"I can go alone. Give the judge the Saji invoice."

"Never mind. I don't have to take any time off. Just give me the ticket. I'll see what I can do."

"Okay. Here, Sheryl, you take it so we don't forget," I hand it over the seat to her.

"Oh, we don't forget things," she answers, grabbing it.

Really? They're that perfect? Do only teens and eighty-two-year-olds experience brain farts? "And here's the invoice, too. Show Officer Wilson I had the car fixed now."

Ron nods. "First thing tomorrow, I'll contact the station. For now, let's forget all about it. Have a pleasant evening."

At an old-age home? He's got to be kidding.

Ron pulls up at the circular driveway and Sheryl helps me out. Susan's knees don't want to hold me, not straight up from a sitting position.

An older man hooked to an IV and bundled in a wheelchair sits in a gazebo just across the driveway. A cigarette hangs from his frown. Surrounding the gazebo are small fir trees decorated with red-and-blue lights and mounds of snow.

Sheryl waves in his direction. "Nice park!" She smiles.

He throws his cigarette to the snow and ignores her.

Real friendly.

"Imagine sitting there and reading a book in the warmer weather," Ron says, as though it's the most beautiful area in the western hemisphere.

The geezer reaches for a packet in his shirt pocket and bangs out another cigarette. Judging by the butts on the snow, it wasn't his first smoke.

"Shall we continue?" Sheryl asks brightly.

We follow her as she leads the march toward the doors, which automatically slide open into a large, bright entrance.

The doors shut behind us, silent and final.

To our right is a cosy sitting area with a little fake fireplace against one wall, complete with Christmas stockings hanging from the mantle. Two ceramic bulldogs with Santa hats on their heads curl up near some overstuffed chairs. A long coffee table stretches in front of a couch. A black globe with silver continents sits in the middle of it. All the places the residents will never get to. A beefy smell wafts through the air, mixed with an undertone of something overly sweet — lilies of the valley, like that lady on the bus. The combo is not a plus.

A lady with large, light brown hair greets us. "Ron, Sheryl ... and you must be Susan!" She reaches out to shake my hand. "I'm Elizabeth. Would you like to tour first or are you hungry?"

"Tour," I answer before my new son and daughter-in-law can.

"Wonderful, I'll just let the kitchen staff know." She pulls out her cellphone and keys something in. "So the grounds aren't much to look at right now, but in the summer we have roses, tulips, lilies, and even some orchids. One of the residents loves gardening so she helps take care of it. Do you like to garden, Susan?"

Oh puke! I don't know. No time to text the real Susan to see. I give a quick look at my nails. They're long and painted a glossy red to match Susan's bright lipstick. "Um, I don't like to get my hands dirty."

"Mother lives on the ninth floor. She doesn't even have a balcony," Sheryl adds, like this place is a big step up.

"So no to gardening then. Don't worry, we have plenty of activities to choose from."

A short bus pulls up at the front now, and the driver jumps out to put a ramp in place.

"Today, some of the residents went to the bank." Elizabeth waves at one of the seniors rolling in with her walker.

The bank, I think. Most boring outing, ever. "Do residents get their own parking spots?"

Elizabeth gives Sheryl a quick look. "As you see, we have buses to take residents out. No one really needs a car."

Double puke! "Out" is a trip to an ATM.

"Some people don't even want to leave. We have a supper club, Bingo, current events, chair yoga, movie night, and a crafts group." She keys a code onto a number pad, which opens the door to another hallway. "If you forget the code, it's written in the box here. That's to keep our wanderers in."

If no one wants to leave, why do they have to know a code to get out?

"This is the Kent Wing. Here's the nursing station." She waves and a lady in white smiles at us. "A full-time nurse makes sure you take all your medications."

That doesn't sound good. I picture some gorilla-sized person stuffing pills down my throat.

"And here is our lounge, where we hold many of our events. Karaoke night, for example." The lounge is a big room where a large-screen TV plays loudly. A few grey-haired people doze on the sofa near it.

"Fun, fun, fun," I say.

She doesn't catch my sarcasm. "You like singing? I always say singing is the soul's way of laughing out loud."

What's laughing then, I wonder. *Singing for the brain?* I shake my head. Neither metaphor really works for me.

We keep walking and she stops to knock on a door. "One of our residents, Andrea, volunteered to show you her room. Andrea? Andrea?" She knocks again and shouts a little louder. "Andrea!" Then she gives up, pulls a key ring from her pocket, and unlocks the door.

For one panicky moment, I imagine Andrea lying dead

on the floor. She has to be pretty old to live here, after all.

The door opens and … no one there. Lucky.

The room looks bigger than my bedroom at home but smaller than our family room. Still, a couch, a media shelf, two bureaus, and a bed are crammed in. My breathing gets faster. Is the furniture closing in on us? And why are there fake flowers in vases everywhere?

"Oh, look at the kitty!" I walk over to a bookshelf where an orange tabby lies curled up. I touch the lifelike fur and the little back rises against my fingers. I jump back. "It's breathing!"

Elizabeth grins. "Battery operated. Isn't that a hoot? No animals are allowed unless they're therapy dogs." She waits while Sheryl admires the robot cat and then continues. "We paint, but of course you are free to decorate your area the way you like."

Decorate? I look around at all the mismatched furniture. Is that what she calls what happened to this room? More like memories of a bigger home.

I open a door that leads to a small washroom with a sink and an industrial-looking toilet, complete with scaffolding around it and a shelf above. A doll in a crocheted pink dress sits over a roll of toilet paper.

"Where's the bathtub and shower?" I ask.

"The shower room is at the end of the hall. You're entitled to two baths or showers a week."

"What!"

"That's by mandate," Elizabeth says. "But of course if you have a family member who wants to help you, you're welcome to have more."

"I shower every day." I look at Sheryl.

"I've heard that North Americans bathe too often. It's not good for us," Sheryl says. "We wash away our pheromones."

"Whatever."

The ladies both stare now.

Uh-oh, I said that outside my head.

Ron tilts his head as though he didn't hear me correctly. "Mom?"

"I don't need pheromones at my age. I want to take a shower whenever I feel like it."

"But you never shower, anyway — you like to take baths." Sheryl raises a concerned eyebrow and aims it at Ron.

"I like showers, now!" I snap. "A person can change her mind."

There's a moment of silence and then Elizabeth changes the subject.

"The room that's coming up for availability has a lovely view of the ravine." She smiles at me.

At this point, I know that if I have to stay in this body at this residence, I will jump into that ravine. I can't smile back.

"This way, please."

She parts a path through a gathering of old people. "Supper hour just ended. Everyone's leaving the dining room." She pushes open one of the doors to a huge area full of tables and chairs. "There's assigned seating, but if you find you don't get along with someone, we can always seat you somewhere else."

The room looks cheery enough. Vases of yellow flowers sit at every table. I rub my fingers over a petal. Thick dusty material; fake, of course. Framed prints of gardens hang from the bandage-coloured walls. As if the pictures can help convince you that all these flowers are real. "Can I eat in my room if I want to?"

"We don't encourage that. If you're sick and have a doctor's letter, we'll deliver your meals for a few days."

And after that, you starve.

Elizabeth leads us to a smaller kitchen where you can volunteer to chop vegetables.

As if.

"Would you like to eat now?" she asks.

Ron nods for all of us and Elizabeth leads us to a private dining room. She tells us we can book this room whenever the family wants to eat with me. I wonder how often that would be. I sure wouldn't want to come here to dine.

A young dude with stiff, glossed curls serves each of us a plate with a breaded cutlet, a pile of mashed potatoes, and carrots. "Gravy with that?" he asks, and when Ron nods again, he ladles it on.

Who needs gravy on a breaded piece of meat? Ron, apparently.

The server smiles down at me. He has these crazy blue eyes and terrific dimples, a dent in his chin as big as a thumbprint.

My heart does a double thump. I shield my food with my hand but I wink at him to show I'm friendly. I smile, too big and wide.

The dude winks back.

Too late, I see Sheryl's horrified look. She nudges Ron.

I'm an eighty-two-year-old flirting with a twenty-something-old server. A perv.

I focus on the meal and sample a little of each. I'm not all that hungry, and it's wall paste, all of it. Bland, bland, bland. I'll have to give Susan a jar of Dad's hot jerk spice. What am I thinking? Susan can't sign up to live in a place like this. Two baths a week, no car. She is an independent lady. I'm going to have to stand firm on this point for her.

CHAPTER 12

Susan

MRS. PRINCE HAS THE SAME WARM skin tone and beautiful lips as Hallie, but it's the moment her arms surround and squeeze me to her that I know the tall woman in the kitchen to be Hallie's mother.

It's love I feel so strongly I can hardly swallow.

My head only reaches her bosom, but Hallie may still grow. If she gets the chance. A warm curry smell wafts around us, and Mariah Carey sings about all that she wants for Christmas over the radio. A bushy over-decorated fir tree sits in the front sitting area, and a long ribbon full of greeting cards hangs in the hall along with four advent calendars. The towels draped over the stove handle are red and green, and there's an evergreen centrepiece on the kitchen table.

"Who was that who drove you home?" Mrs. Prince asks, with a slight edge of suspicion.

"Susan. She's my adopted grandmother. An empathy project for school," I answer. The lie feels like truth by now, anyway. "I'm supposed to learn what it's like to be old and help her with technology." And maybe it *is* all an empathy project, only it belongs to Eli. He's the one who will decide if we pass or fail it all.

I don't want to answer a lot of questions until I'm more comfortable with Hallie's identity. Otherwise, Mrs. Prince will catch on that her daughter has changed. So I head out of the kitchen again. "Uh, I'm going to go tidy my room now."

"Say what?" Hallie's mother asks. Already, her eyes narrow. "Did you say 'tidy'?"

"You want me to clean my bedroom, don't you?"

"Well, yeah! But I haven't even nagged you about it yet."

"Okay, well ... I'm maturing, I guess." I grin at my little inside joke. If only Mrs. Prince knew just how much more mature her daughter has become since this morning.

I leave the kitchen. *Now, which way is Hallie's room?* I wonder and start back to the front, where I noticed stairs earlier. Second floor, I'm guessing, and climb up. With no one around, it's safe for me to explore and open each door. When I hit the bathroom, I use it. Then right next to it is a linen closet and after that a bedroom that looks like a hurricane hit it, and not the Saji Motors kind. To make absolutely certain the room belongs to Hallie, I step inside and lift a pair of jeans from the unmade bed, holding them close to my hips. Yes siree, a fit. I begin to gather and pile all the dirty clothes in one corner. Beneath some underwear on a bureau, I discover a framed photo of Abby and Hallie, so I must have the right room.

There are some pizza crusts under the bed, along with some crumpled potato chip bags. Using the little waste bin I found in the bathroom, I dispose of all that. Then I gather the clothes pile in my arms. "Mom! Where do we keep the laundry detergent?"

"In the basement with the washer and dryer, like always!" Hallie's mother calls back.

I stagger down the two flights of stairs with the mountain of Hallie's dirty clothes. In the basement family room, I see a young girl on a couch, perhaps seven or eight, with paler skin than Hallie, ginger pompom pigtails, and green eyes like her mom's and sister's. "You're blocking the television," she complains to me.

"So-rree!" I stagger on through a passage to a small cinder-block alcove, the laundry room. There I stuff the washer with Hallie's clothes, adding the detergent from the shelf just above it, press numerous buttons, and listen to an electronic melody signalling the start. A broom with a dustpan attached to the stick and a box of garbage bags sits next to the dryer. Technology that I understand.

I climb up the stairs again with this cleaning equipment, barely feeling my knees at all. I should be breathless and exhausted but instead I feel invigorated. Ah, to be young! To stay young forever! This different ending to my life is wonderful.

Back upstairs, I sweep out the dustballs in Hallie's room and empty the bathroom garbage. Some magazines get shelved, the shoes get lined up. I decide to change the bed. Down the stairs again, I'm in time to put the wash in the dryer and then toss in the sheets.

"Hallie! Come and set the table!" Mrs. Prince calls down to me.

I stomp up to the kitchen, still breathing easy and grinning.

At that moment, the El-Q plays music from my bag. It's a text from Abby.

What cha doin?

Laundry, I answer.

No really? Abby texts back.

Cleaning my room and laundry. Setting the table.

You're such a kidder. Wanna hang out tomorrow?

Sure.

Doing what?

Tomorrow is my Aquafit class, which usually helps make my hips and knees work more smoothly. But my joints are in premium shape in this body. I don't need to water jog. Still, this week is a special Christmas coffee and brunch afterward and all my friends will be there; I will miss celebrating with people my own age. Wait a minute! After Aquafit is a 60s Swing and Swim for teens, free because of the holiday. I remember Linda telling me she wished she were young enough to go.

Why don't we go swimming at Tansley Woods? Free tomorrow.

Who else is going? Abby asks.

I'll text Chael and Hardeep.

Really?

Too forward? But I need to act fast. How long can I possibly stay fifteen?

And Megan, I add, remembering that contact name on my El-Q.

OK. What time?

One o'clock.

"Hallie? The table please! Put down your toy."

"Sorry, Mom." I put the El-Q back in my bag. "Smells wonderful." I select the wrong drawer to find cutlery but cover up by handing Mrs. Prince the ladle she will need in a minute to serve up. From the next drawer over, I pull out the knives and forks. "Do we have napkins?"

"Napkins?" Mrs. Prince squints at me. "Just put the paper towel roll on the table."

When I'm finished laying out the forks and knives at every chair, I stand waiting for Hallie's mother to hand me the plates full of food.

"My, my. You are helpful today. What big-ticket item are you wanting for Christmas?" Mrs. Prince hands me two plates full of rice and curried chicken. "Call your sister up from the basement."

I don't need notes on how to do this; my mind is so sharp, I remember how kids do this from my own two. I just open the door to the basement and yell loudly and obnoxiously, "Aria! Come up for dinner."

Mrs. Prince rolls her eyes. "I could have done that myself."

Truer words have never been spoken.

I sit down at the setting farthest from the cooking area. The close one has to be Mrs. Prince's seat. Mothers usually do all the jumping up and serving.

Hallie's little sister finally bounces in. She sits at the setting next to mine, but the moment she sees what's on the plates, she whines about the food. "Why can't we have fried or barbecued chicken? I hate curry."

I scoop up a mouthful. "Mmm." I can't help myself. "I love it."

Both Aria and her mother give me a stare.

"Well, it's especially delicious today, you have to admit. Come on, Aria, just try it!"

"You're being weird," Aria answers but takes a spoonful.

Teenagers eat quickly and don't answer a lot of questions, as I remember it. "How's your day?" "How is your room coming?" What's new?" can all be answered with two words. *Okay* and *nothing*.

Aria chatters away, instead.

When everyone seems done, I clear the dishes to the sink, rinse them, and begin to load them into the dishwasher. Over the clatter, I don't notice the silence these actions cause till Aria shouts.

"You're not Hallie! What have you done with my sister?"

The hair at the back of my neck prickles. I've been found out.

"Stop that!" Mrs. Prince answers. "Hallie is working on a project. Now why don't you develop some empathy, too, by wiping the table."

For the rest of the evening, I hide in Hallie's room and text invites to the 60s swim event at the pool. Everyone says yes. The real Hallie will be so pleased that Chael is coming.

The real Hallie. Hmm. I try calling her on the El-Q, but she never answers. So I text. I know I'm supposed to be brief; this isn't like snail mail so I keep it to four sentences. Four sentences when I have so many more things to say.

You need to go to Aquafit at noon tomorrow at Tansley Woods. Bathing suit and towel is in bathroom closet at the condo. Afterwards hang around. I'm going to try to get you that boyfriend.

CHAPTER 13

Hallie

"NAH! I DON'T WANT TO COME IN. Thanks anyway." Last thing I need after the tour of Sunnyside Terrace and a silent drive toward their house is to go in and visit with Sheryl and Ron to discuss the residence.

Sheryl raises an eyebrow at Ron, a pointy, judgemental eyebrow. I can almost guess that she's awarding me ten points on the senior-unreasonable-dementia scale.

"I'm tired," I explain. "I need my beauty rest." That's something Mom tells me all the time so it's as close to senior-speak as I can get.

"But we need to make a decision quickly," Sheryl insists. "Once the family cleans out that poor woman's belongings from the room overlooking the ravine, there'll be a lineup for it."

Poor woman? Dead poor woman? I think about the see-through people that were at the carnival. Is she one of them? Someone riding that teacup ride or merry-go-round?

"It's a lot to take in." Ron seems to be on my side. He helps me out of the back seat of their Blizzard and into the driver's seat of my own car. "But Mom, we can't delay this forever." He kisses me on the cheek and I give him a little wave. Then I shut the door.

Huh! I will never treat my mother like that. Tricking her into visiting a residence with a fake dinner invitation.

As I switch on the El-Q to use the GPS, a text from Susan flashes up. Something about Aquafit ... and Chael. How she thinks she's going to land him, I don't know. I just hope I'm back in my own body to enjoy her success. The Hurricane drives smoothly as I navigate the turns to get to Susan's condo. When I arrive, I park right in the front without using the assist feature. I could probably pass my driving test today if they allowed me to take it. Then I head slowly for the door so as not to strain my old knees and ankles. Just inside are a couple of grey-haired ladies sitting on a bench. One wears a red jacket and clashing fuchsia slacks with large, white sneakers that look like moon boots. She smiles as I come in. "Good evening, Susan, did you have a nice dinner?"

"Yes, thank you," I lie. None of their business, anyways.

The other lady smirks like she knows the secret to the world as she holds on to a cane propped between her knees. Underneath an open camel-haired coat, she wears a blue floral top that ends at the knees of her denim pants. Those pants stop just short of a pair of ugly, black lace-up boots. Kind of mismatched and style free — things Abby might buy at a thrift shop and look creative and funky in. Not these ladies, though.

"You know you're not allowed to park in the front. Those spots are reserved for visitors," the cane lady says.

I sooo hope I am just visiting, I think and sigh. "Where am I supposed to park?" It's hard pretending to be another person, especially when every joint aches and I'm bone tired.

"In your spot in the underground lot, of course."

How will I know where the spot is? I fumble for my El-Q to try to Q-Time Susan but she doesn't seem to be online. "I'm having a hard day, can you just …"

"Rules are for everybody. You can't just park willy-nilly wherever you like."

"But that indoor garage can be a nuisance," the lady in red and fuchsia argues. "Susan's driving out tomorrow morning, anyway."

How does she know that?

"That doesn't matter. What if my son wants to visit me and there are no spots left?"

"Wouldn't he call first? And doesn't he just pick you up at the front door?"

"Shut up!"

Both of them look at me, shocked.

I hold my fist to my forehead. "I have a terrible headache." Scrambling through Susan's purse, I find keys and they're marked Unit 909.

I turn from the women on the bench. They continue talking as I walk away.

"Really, Margret, maybe you shouldn't have bothered her about the car. She seems so upset."

"Linda. I simply do not care. Someone has to keep people on track around here."

Do they just assume everyone's deaf? I leave the building and get back in the Hurricane. Then I drive it to what I now see is the garage door — if only I knew how to open it.

A silver pickup truck with oversized tires pulls up behind me and honks, twice.

"Is there some problem, Mrs. MacMillan?" A disembodied voice comes from a speaker on a short pole to the left of the entrance.

"Yes. I can't open the garage."

"Your key fob not working?" the voice asks.

Ah! That's it. I wave my key at the unit underneath the speaker and the door lifts.

"Seems to be working now," I tell the speaker and slowly drive ahead. The truck follows on my bumper as I inch forward, hoping for some clue as to where to pull in.

Painted in large red numbers on the cement wall is 909. *Phew!* This time I switch on the park assist and throw the Hurricane in neutral. Eerily, the computer takes over, lining up the car with the others, backing in, and finally beeping its success and turning itself off. The truck, meanwhile, swerves around and screeches to its own parking spot. *Everyone's in a hurry*, I think.

I follow a heavyset man with rust-coloured hair and sideburns from the truck to the elevator.

"Ever thought of changing the battery in your key fob, Mrs. MacMillan?" he says.

"Have you ever thought of trying chair yoga?" I snap back. He needs to take some kind of chill pill.

"Like I've got time between shifts." He punches the seventh and ninth floor buttons. "Less than an hour to eat and change before I start delivering pizza." The door slides open on the seventh and he sprints out.

"Have a nice evening!" I call after him. The elevator stops on the ninth floor and I walk to the end of the hall, counting numbers. My first apartment ever. I expected to be sharing it with Abby or Megan, to have parties every night or at least stay out late and not have to answer to my parents.

And here it is, 909 — I unlock and open the door, sighing — in spectacular beige and cream with big red roses all over the couches. What is it with old people and flowers? A dark brown wooden floor leads through to the galley kitchen, which has matching dark oak cabinets. A bit coffin-like, if you ask me. The windows look out over twinkling lights. They end in inky blackness that might be the lake. Different than how I'd planned but still a place all for myself! Maybe better than Susan's credit card or car.

I check out the bathroom. Oh yeah, a Jacuzzi tub! No wonder Susan doesn't like to shower. The walls are the shade of masking tape, and on top of a dark wooden cabinet sits one of those bowl sinks. The mirror slides open to a medicine cabinet. A glass on the counter reminds me of my Uncle Bill, who keeps his teeth in one back at the farm. Panicking, I slam the mirror shut and lean close, opening my mouth wide to see if Susan's teeth are real. They don't look perfectly straight or white. I dig a finger-nail into the gum and feel it. Just to make sure, I slide open the mirror and check the shelves. No denture cream there. But there are vials of pills with Susan's name on them and instructions on how to take them. Just how sick is she? I'll have to ask her about that.

Next door, the spare room has a large desk surrounded on three walls by shelves — some hold books, others knick-knacks. A tall giraffe sits on one, a large elephant on another. Did Susan bring these home from Africa? She has this whole life I have to fake but know nothing about.

Then the bedroom. It's huge and still beige with thick, coffee-coloured carpeting that springs back beneath my sneakers. I want to sink my bare feet into it, so I unlace Susan's sneakers, kick them off, and pull down her ankle socks.

Oh my god! Skeleton feet! These toes are long and bumpy, with thick, yellow nails, too. Quickly, I roll the socks back up, fling myself on the bed, and hyperventilate for a few moments. When my breath evens out, I realize this bed is gigantic, and across from me, there's a second bathroom. Two bathrooms just for me. I won't have to share with Aria or anyone. When one's dirty, I can just switch to the other.

Next to the bathroom door sits a dresser, and on it, a huge TV. My own bathrooms, my own personal viewing station! I pick up the remote and turn it on. I can watch all night if I like, which is why Mom doesn't allow us to have TVs in our rooms. Today, my eyes feel heavy and it's only nine thirty. Better see if I can get hold of Susan and find out about those pills in the bathroom medicine cabinet. I touch the El-Q face button and then touch Susan's profile shot. A couple of warbles later, I see my former self on the screen, smiling. I miss my unwrinkled young skin, never mind my plump feet. There's a smaller image of Susan in the corner. The Susan I'm stuck inside.

"Hi there. Just want to say your place is amazing!"

"Glad you like it," Susan answers. "I cleaned your room so I hope you keep my condo tidy."

"Um, sure." I look around. So far, just a purse and shoes are flung across the floor; the condo could still be described as neat. "Listen, I saw a lot of pills in your medicine cabinet. Can you give me the lowdown on what to take?"

"Certainly. For now, there's a pillbox labelled with the days of the week. When we're done on the El-Q, you need to take Monday PM. Have a glass of milk with it. Tomorrow, you need to take both Tuesday AM and PM. The AM with breakfast. The PM with dinner."

"Okay. What's this about Aquafit?"

"Well, tomorrow is a special holiday potluck for the regulars. Margret and Linda will want a lift."

"You're kidding. Those busybodies that sit at the entrance?"

She grins. "Oh, they're not as bad as all that. Margret's husband passed just last year and she's taking it hard. We play rummy cube on Wednesday nights together. They're pretty big gamblers."

"And what's this about you and Chael? How do you know if he's even going to be there?"

"I invited him and he said yes."

"He did!" I squeal in an old lady's voice. "That has to mean he likes me … don't you think?"

"Of course he does, dear. Sometimes you just need to let a person know that you're interested. So don't forget those pills. Is there anything you want me to know about?"

So much, I don't know where to begin. I look around her huge bedroom and suddenly remember Andrea's claustrophobic room at the residence. "You know how Ron and Sheryl invited you to dinner? Well, they actually surprised me with a tour and a meal at Sunnyside Terrace."

"How dreadful. They really are pushing this home on me. What was it like?"

I purse my thin pale lips but in the end can't stop the thought from going vocal. "You'd probably rather die."

CHAPTER 14

Susan

LYING IN BED, TRYING NOT TO wake up, I can't help noticing that my condo is very noisy this morning. Traffic news blares from a radio somewhere. "Eastbound QEW is backed up from Trafalgar, where a tractor-trailer has overturned. Westbound …" A door slams.

My eyes flutter. Things look different.

"Where are my gym shorts?" someone yells.

What is going on? I open my eyes wide and sit up in an unfamiliar bed. Where am I?

I yawn and stretch wide. Despite the strange surroundings, last night's sleep was the best I have had in a long time, no waking up to go to the bathroom and no tossing and turning till dawn. I roll out of bed and feel no aches and pains. That's when I remember. This is Hallie's room.

A whole household bustles around me.

I rush to the bathroom and knock hard on the door because, at this point, I desperately need to use the toilet.

A man's voice calls out, "Give me a second, honey … Okay, come on in."

Clearly, I'm expected to do my business while Hallie's father showers. I step in and quickly sit down on the toilet, nearly falling because the lid is up. After shutting it, I re-seat myself, all the while trying not to look at the profile of a man outlined on the shower curtain. The steamy room smells of some kind of spiced citrus aftershave. I shudder; toilet lids up and aftershave all remind me of my former husband, Ron Senior, who ran off when the children were toddlers. When I'm done, I flush.

Mr. Prince hollers out in dismay.

"Ah! Sorry. I forgot." I hope I haven't scalded him.

Hallie's father peaks his head around the curtain, his skin looking almost as red as his hair.

"Sorry!" I repeat and he ducks his head back in. How can I brush my teeth and not scald him again? I'll have to wait, I suppose. This is why I like living alone back in my real life, why I don't move in with my children. Too much happening.

I wipe a spot of steam from the mirror and notice a dark spot in the middle of my forehead. Touching it, I realize it's hard and tender at the same time. A pimple! I can't remember the last time I've had one of those. Things have changed so much, there must be something I can do for this. Is there not an app on the El-Q that zaps them? I pull a few strands of hair forward. Better already. That's the ticket! I will pull down some strands of Hallie's hair into bangs. Maybe a hairband will help and add that certain 60s touch to my do. I can fashion one out of a scarf if I can find one.

"See you!" I call to the profile on the shower curtain and then return to my room.

It seems that all of Hallie's clothes are stored on the floor, as there is no underwear in any of her bureau drawers. I sigh and decide I will dress straight from the dryer. That's what teens do, I expect. Fuzzy teeth, scrambling for clothes … I miss the quiet routine of my condo, a newspaper in my hands, a cup of coffee. On the way past the kitchen, I spy a Brewmaster and feel relieved that I won't have to miss this vestige of civilization. I reach for a cup, pour myself some, and sip. *Ahhh!*

"You're drinking coffee this morning?" Mrs. Prince sneaks up on me from out of nowhere.

I jump and nearly spill the rest. That's right. Hallie didn't order coffee at lunch yesterday. I fumble to cover for myself. "Is it okay, Mom? I feel a bit dopey and thought it would wake me up."

"Are you all right, Hallie?" Mrs. Prince asks, frowning. "Abby's mom called this morning. She says a car knocked you down yesterday."

I take a moment and a breath. Last thing I want is to be taken to the doctor for any kind of checkup; I might end up in the psychiatric ward. "It barely nudged me." I head for the fridge and remove the egg carton. "I was texting and fell down from the shock is all."

"But you didn't go to the hospital to have yourself looked at." Mrs. Prince squints as I place a couple of eggs in a saucepan and fill it with water. "What are you doing?"

"Making myself a boiled egg. Would you like one?" I set the pot on the stove and turn the element on. The moment I turn around, I realize that I've made another blunder.

"You never eat eggs!" Mrs. Prince walks over to me and cups my chin in her hand. "You must have knocked your head."

For just one moment, I find myself leaning into her hand, smiling. It's nice to have a mother's touch; I haven't had that for thirty years. "I'm fine, Mom. Honestly. Would you just set the timer for five minutes? I really want my eggs soft boiled."

"No Frosted Flakes?" She snaps her head back, furrows her brow. "Fine. Go get dressed."

I pick up my coffee cup again and continue down to the laundry room. There, I search through the dryer, flinging clothes to the counter. What if Hallie only wears thongs? While I long to brush my teeth all by myself in the bathroom, I don't want to floss my derriere anywhere.

I gulp at the coffee in between flings. Ah-ha! What's this? A nice pair of cotton spandex Wonder Woman briefs. And a tiny bra, so cute! I pull on some blue spandex leggings and a long-sleeved red top. Huh. Now, what about a bathing suit?

I hum as I fold Hallie's clothing and hunt for one. In my head, I hear the words, "She wore an itsy-bitsy teeny-weeny yellow polka-dot bikini ..." I was in my twenties when the song came out, and Ron Senior, my husband at the time, wouldn't let me wear one. But today, if I find a yellow polka-dotted bikini, I know it will work with the retro theme at the pool as well as accentuate my great complexion. Another swallow, and I finish both the coffee and the folding. Despite a tower of tops and pants, still no bikini. I hook my cup handle over my fingers as I carry the tower in a basket back up the stairs.

"Eggs are done when you're ready," Mrs. Prince calls. "What, you folded your clothes?" she says as I walk past her.

I pull out another teenaged move I remember from my kids. "Duh. How else am I gonna put my clothes away?" I roll my eyes.

Mrs. Prince's eyebrows raise.

I shrug and continue to Hallie's room.

When I spot myself in the mirror above the bureau, I cringe. Why does Hallie own these unflattering tight things; no wonder she thinks her thighs are heavy. I hunt and find a faded, torn pair of jeans and throw them over-top. The last time I was fifteen, blue denim was considered farming wear. Now, it seems, the more worn out the bet-ter. It screams I don't really care what I wear. So much more freedom nowadays, fashion and otherwise.

I sigh, happy to have this extra chance to enjoy it. As I tuck the laundry away in the drawers, I hunt again for that bikini. Nowhere. In desperation, I check the closet and find something underneath some flip-flops on the floor, of all places. It's an orange tankini with unfortu-nate boy-cut shorts that would turn any pair of legs into barrel staves. The top dips down daringly in the front, but Hallie's body doesn't have much cleavage. Rather, her breasts are small and perky — I never had such stand-up little soldiers, not even when I was twelve. The top works, though. I stuff them in the backpack along with a towel from the linen closet. Then I grab my El-Q and head to the kitchen again.

Mrs. Prince has set the eggs in little chicken holders.

"Thanks, Mom," I say. "Any coffee left?"

"You already had one cup. Have orange juice this time. You don't want to be stunting your growth."

"Okay." Of course, in my older body, the doctor routinely makes me swear off caffeine for the sake of my heart. Maybe there are only twenty good years in your life when you can eat and drink as you like, and even then, if you're pregnant or nursing, you have to deny yourself certain foods and alcohol. I remember now, too, that I can't drive myself around in this young body. I must text Hallie for the bus route numbers the next chance I get. For now I ask Mrs. Prince. "Uh … Mom" — the word feels warm and soothing on my tongue — "can you take me to Tansley Woods Pool for one o'clock?"

"If you don't mind being early, I can drop you off. I have an appointment at a salon nearby at twelve thirty. "

"Sure. My adoptive grandmother will be in Aquafit then. Maybe I can visit with her," I look around for a newspaper to read while I eat my egg. Nothing.

A soft ding from my El-Q signals an email coming in. *Who could that be?* I wonder as I touch the little envelope picture. Turns out it's a note from Hallie telling me she's joined the Saji Happy Motoring Club. The username is *Gran* and the password *Naturaldisasters*. I should test it out and have a look around.

Immediately, I visit the site, logging in with the information Hallie gave me.

I notice that if I had booked a winter tire change back in November when my body still belonged to that of an eighty-two-year-old, I could have had a free scraper and brush. Too late — besides, I have all-season tires; those should be good enough. In the corner of the screen is a button I can click on to download a *Saji Motoring* magazine PDF. Maybe later. Then, a red bar pops up across the middle of the page, inviting me to hit enter so I can win a trip for two to Japan. I can do that. Of course, I don't know if I'll be around to enjoy that prize, but I fill out the entry anyway, picturing Hallie and me perhaps travelling together. My pretend granddaughter is starting to become very real to me. I pause and smile for a moment.

Then I go to something called the "Community Forum" and search the message board.

Do any other drivers have problems? I wonder.

Someone called Sport comments on the moon roof sticking halfway.

Crazypants complains of a fishy smell in his late-model Tornado.

Blah, blah, blah. Then I spot another message that makes my heart double beat.

Yesterday, the accelerator stuck. Just for a minute but way scary. Anyone else have that happen? HOTROD

I want to wave and shout, "I did!" The harrowing drive along the QEW flashes through my mind: poor inexperienced Hallie steering madly to avoid the school bus, the children innocently waving from the back window all the while. Hallie inadvertently cutting off the minivan, throwing the dog hanging from the window to the back when the driver swerved. Hallie finally pulling to the shoulder, only to face a motorcyclist, Santa-biker no less. I had been sure we were going to hit him and send him flying.

Yes, I type. I take a breath. *My Hurricane's gas pedal stuck. But it's been fixed. GRAN.*

The Hurricanes have that problem too? I drive a Blizzard. HOTROD

I shiver, suddenly cold. Could it be? I have to warn Ron. He has never complained about unintended acceleration, but he does drive a Blizzard. That horror scene on the QEW could still happen to him. Only perhaps with a worse ending, this time.

CHAPTER 15

Hallie

BLAM, BLAM, BLAM! I MASH A PILLOW over my head. Why is someone hammering so early in the morning? Christmas holidays, after all. I'm allowed sleeping in, especially since I'm eighty-two now. Someone's calling in the distance. "Susan, Susan!"

I ignore it. The clock on the bedside table reads 10:00. Plenty of time before Aquafit. I drift off again, dreaming I'm on a carousel, riding in some kind of open car. Suddenly, it moves too fast, swirling, everything a blur.

Blam, blam, blam! The hammering forces me to leave the carousel. My eyelids unstick and stay open this time. The noise sounds louder and closer now.

"Susan, Susan. Open up!"

I sit up. What can anyone want from a senior at this hour in the morning?

Then I hear a key rattling in my door.

Luckily, I'm still in yesterday's clothes because, before I can grab a bathrobe, three people rush into my bedroom, one of them a tall man.

"What are you doing still in bed?" that bossy lady from the front bench says, shaking a rolled newspaper at me. "Why are you wearing clothes?"

Margret, that's her name, I think as my brain slowly awakens.

"Um, I was too tired to change."

Linda, the clashing-colours woman, gives me a frownie face. "We thought you had a heart attack!"

I stare open-mouthed at the three of them. Linda wears sky-blue sweat pants with a kiwi-coloured winter jacket. She's carrying a tray of coffee in one hand and one of those house-shaped boxes of doughnut bits in the other. Both Linda and Margret wear clear plastic bonnets over their heads, the kind I've only seen folded up accordion-style before.

The tall dude looks sheepishly at me from beneath long bangs. He holds a ring of keys in his hand, a long flash-light hanging from some kind of leather tool belt around his waist. "They were awful worried about you, Mrs. MacMillan. Glad you're okay," He backs out of the room. "I'll leave you all to it."

"Are you not feeling well?" Linda says, handing me a coffee.

"No, I'm exhausted. I had to get up to go to the bath-room a million times in the night. Then I woke up at five and couldn't get back to sleep."

Linda's head tilts. "So why didn't you do your word search? When we walked the hall at six, we saw you hadn't even taken the paper in."

"You always take it in by the time we pass," Margret says.

How does she know this? Do they parade the halls that early every morning? I shudder. "I just wanted to stay in bed!"

"In the middle of the week? Get up now," Margret barks. "We brought sour cream bits."

"You're still driving us to the pool, aren't you?" Linda asks. "We want to get there early for the potluck."

"Get out!" I wave with my arms and then add, "So I can get dressed!"

They shuffle into the hall and I try to jump out of bed. *Ow, ow!* Feels like someone took a baseball bat to my knees and ankles. I sit back down and rub my legs. When I finally make it up, I walk tin-man style to the bedroom door and slam it after them.

Then I strip and accidentally catch sight of my Susan body in the mirror. *Gah!* Bony feet, blue-veined legs, ripples of white belly flesh, flappy arms, and awful pancake boobs. I never had the chance to appreciate my young ones, and now I'm stuck with these saggy ones.

And if I don't figure out what Eli wants from me, I may be stuck in this body forever. Or worse.

It takes me a long time to coordinate a pair of beige pants with a non-flowered shirt. I hate flowers and polka-dots in all sizes and that's all Susan seems to own. Finally, I find a leopard print and wear that. I pull on some see-through nylon sock things and hunt for Susan's sneakers. One's under the bed, the other behind the door. I sip at the black coffee Linda left me. Pills. *Must take the Tuesday AM pills*, I think, and head for the bathroom. There's some "sensitive" toothpaste. I brush and then grab the long rectangle of little windows labelled Monday AM through to Sunday PM.

I touch the Saturday box — Christmas falls on Saturday this year. Only four days away now. My favourite time of the year.

Christmas Eve, Dad will brine the turkey with chili powder and garlic.

Mom will make a wild rice stuffing and a mashed sweet potato casserole.

Christmas morning we'll open presents before a cinnamon French toast breakfast. The house will be filled with delicious smells. Aunt Claire, Uncle Bill, and my cousins Layla, Kae, and Raene will come and bring some awful fruit cake. We'll eat and then sing "Silent Night," "Away in a Manger," and all the classics, to Dad's accordion. Having my family around me always feels like a day-long hug.

Only I won't make it if I'm stuck in this body.

I shake my head. There's nothing I can do except hope for the best so I pop open Tuesday AM and dump the bunch of pills into my other hand. Then I head to the dining area.

They're sitting there waiting, coats over their chairs.

"You certainly took your sweet time," Margret says. "Have some breakfast." She pushes the doughnut box toward me. "You know how you get when you don't eat with those pills."

I grab a couple of the doughnut bits and chow down. Mmm, way better than my usual Frosted Flakes. Then I take another swig of my coffee and swallow the pills. They stick in my throat till I take a few more gulps of caffeine and throw my head back.

"How is the Hurricane? Any more episodes?" Linda asks.

She knows, I think. How much more should I tell her? "The problem's been fixed," I finally say.

"Did you make anything for the potluck?" Margret asks.

"Were we supposed to?"

"You said you were going to make your Confetti Salad. You always make it for potlucks."

"Doesn't matter." Linda pats my hand. "There's probably way too much food."

"We'll bring the rest of these, then." Margret tucks the corners of the doughnut box closed, then unrolls the newspaper, dividing it up, handing me the word search. The theme is Remembering.

She clicks a ballpoint pen and attacks the crossword. "What's a six-letter word for imperfection?"

"Do you have a clue for us?" Linda asks.

"Down is 'A calamitous event,' eight letters."

"That's a toughie," Linda says.

In the meantime, I find and circle the word *automobile* and *manufacturer*. Can't think what that has to do with the memory theme except it makes me remember the Hurricane speeding out of control yesterday. "Defect," I suddenly say out loud. "For across, I mean. An imperfection is a defect."

"That could be it," Linda nods. "It's six letters."

"What's the calamitous event then?" Margret asks. "It would have to start with a *D*."

"Disaster!" All the Saji cars are named after disasters.

We complete the whole crossword together and I finish the word search. The letters left uncircled in the puzzle spell *recall*. When you remember something, I suppose you do "recall" it. But the word makes me think more about the Hurricane. Does anyone else have a gas pedal that sticks? Should Saji Motors be charging for extra repairs to fix the problem or should there be a recall?

By now the ladies want to pack up and head over to the community centre. Apparently, Linda has a large-print book version of the latest award winner on reserve. "Only one available in all the branches."

"You could just get yourself an e-reader and make every book a large print. They even loan them out," I tell her. "Just a minute. Let me show you my new El-Q." I head for the bedroom, grab my device from the night table, and bring it to the dining room. "Here, look." I touch open the sample book that came with it. Then I press the plus sign for the font.

Linda gasps. "That is wonderful. How did you find out about this?"

"I have a new project: an empathy granddaughter. She teaches me all about technology."

"How much did you pay for that?" Margret asks.

"The El-Q was six hundred and change. The techie grandchild is free. Maybe we should get you one." I stand up. "Come on, let's go."

"Do you have your bag? Your lock? Your medication?" Margret barks as she and Linda put on their coats.

While her questions annoy me, they also happen to be helpful. Susan's Aquafit bag is in the bathroom closet — that was in her El-Q message. I rummage through it and find a lock, some flip-flops, a gigantic black one-piece, but no towel. I grab one from the rack, then get Susan's purse from the bedroom. "Ready."

Linda picks up Susan's coat from the couch, where I threw it last night.

"Careless," Margret grumbles and clicks her tongue.

Linda holds it up for me to put my arms through. With their eyes on me, I shuffle through Susan's keys to get the correct one to lock the door.

And we're off! I know the way to Tansley Woods and I don't use the expressway. I'm careful to stop at red lights and stop signs, check both ways. When the El-Q burps, I ignore it, even though Margret offers to check for me.

At the last intersection, when my foot pushes down a little harder, I feel a sudden surge. After the push rather than during. Delayed, unconnected? *Defect, disaster, recall.* Am I just feeling paranoid after working on those puzzles? I take my foot off the gas, press the brake. The car jerks to a stop.

Margret, beside me, snaps forward and frowns at me.

Did the accelerator stick again? I wonder. The voice in my head screams *yes*, but I ignore both it and Margret, move my foot from the brake to the accelerator, easy, easy, and we move slowly forward.

I honk when I see Chael and Hardeep crossing the street. Then I see their puzzled looks when I wave.

"Do you know those young men?" Linda asks.

Whoops. "Um, I thought I did. Mixed them up with someone else."

We turn into the Tansley Woods parking lot. Linda immediately heads to the library for her book on hold. Margret and I go to the party room and put the little house of doughnut bits on the long table in the centre of it.

It's a sad room with windowless pale-green walls and metal folding chairs arranged along all of them. Not much party to it except for the reindeer paper tablecloth and a cheery senior who dashes in with a Santa hat, singing "Here comes Santa Claus, here comes Santa Claus." He's carrying a large metal bowl.

Someone in black spandex sets up a pile of red paper dishes and opens a bag of plastic cutlery. These she arranges in Styrofoam cups along the edge of the table. The moment she's done, she snatches up one of our sour cream bits. The cheerful Santa man sets down his bowl, which contains a opinach salad.

"Good afternoon, girls," he calls. "Ho-ho-ho. Have you been naughty or nice?" He winks, and if I were still in a fifteen-year-old body, it might be creepy.

Instead, I chuckle nervously and answer, "N-nice."

Another person sets a plate of shaped shortbread down. Reindeer, bells, Christmas trees, and stars, all iced and oprinkled I grab a bell.

"You think your gall bladder can take that?" Margret asks. "After those doughnut bits?"

I'm chewing by the time I hear her warning, so I finish the bell anyway and sneak a few stars and trees into my bag for later, seeing as I don't really know how to cook. *What does a gall bladder even do?* I wonder.

We join Linda in the changing room and I see a lot of pale-skinned ladies changing into their suits out in the open. They seem happy with their floppy bits hanging out for all to see. Not me. I hide in a cubicle so I can re-shock myself with my old body in private. Happily, there's no mirror, and I rush to put on the black bathing suit that doesn't hide nearly enough of the sags and wrinkles. Back outside, I shower and head for the pool.

I haven't been to Tansley Woods pool since last summer. It's large, divided by a double-loop waterslide and an island with three tired-looking artificial palm trees. Tall floor-to-ceiling windows separate the pool from an indoor playground on one side and bright winter sunshine on the other. Along another wall, the windows offer spectator viewing from the community centre.

The grey-haired exercise gang and I get into the pool and face toward those windows — and a high-wattage lady with a wide hairband and a booming voice. The music pumps out nice and loud. Elvis sings about being "all shook up," and I sure know how he feels. The Santa senior who put out the spinach salad belts out the words as he wiggles to the lady's moves.

Watching him makes me laugh out loud, and he winks at me.

Ew! Flirting with a geezer.

We water jog, ski, do some crunches, noodle weight-lifting — none of it very aerobic but still I'm exhausted. It's hard work being old. Through the windows I see some familiar faces, and this time I remember to hold myself back from waving. Chael points to the Santa man and laughs.

I want to shield the flirty, funny, old guy — and kick Chael.

Hardeep shrugs.

Beside him I see myself, at least my old self. I look amazing! I'm wearing an orange hairband over bangs and I'm smiling — and so happy ... er ... Susan looks so happy. Her eyes shine, her smile stretches wide.

After class finishes, Susan walks onto the deck in my tankini. She's pinned the shorts up so that they angle into a point along the sides, showing more of my legs. They don't look bad at all.

I head over to her.

"Did you get my message?" Susan asks me.

"No. I was driving. What did you say?"

"It's about the message board on Saji Happy Motoring. There's a person who calls himself Hotrod. His Blizzard races away on him, too."

"Really? So it's not just the Hurricane."

"We have to warn Ron," she says.

"Right! Do you think he'll even listen?"

"That's the problem, isn't it? I just don't know." Susan frowns.

A voice calls out, interrupting us. "Hey, thunder thighs!" Chael, of course. Alongside Hardeep, his legs look miles long. They head toward us from the men's changing room. Susan hesitates for a moment. Then she strides over to him, her frown changing into a wonky grin. Whispers something into his ear. Chael's skin flushes. She must be telling him something good. She leans back and I know she's up to something. Everyone else seems to know it, too. The pool area gets so quiet you can hear a wave slap on the wall. Until the splash.

CHAPTER 16

Susan

CHAEL'S EARS STICK OUT JUST like Ron Senior's, my ex-husband, so I find myself more irritated by him than I should be, young and handsome as he is. His big grin is knowing and teasing all at the same time, and his laughing eyes make me feel like I'm part of one of his inside jokes. When Chael calls out that insult about my legs, it takes a moment for me to figure out what to do. Then I stroll toward him, flashing my best smile.

May as well take advantage of Hallie's beautiful teeth and lips.

Chael's ears will be sensitive; Ron Senior's always were. If I blow air gently against one before I whisper into it, Chael will feel a light tickling sensation.

I touch his shoulder and lean in; he leans in, too, anticipating ... I sigh into my cupped hand at his ear. "My legs ..."

He smiles.

"... are perfect the way they are!" I step back and lift my right leg, feeling the vigour of youth. Then I push my heel up and connect with his derriere, kicking him into the pool.

Emerging from the water, sputtering, he curses. "What's the matter with you?"

I don't dignify that question with a response. Instead, I shake my finger at him. "Don't you ever comment on my body again!"

Hallie just stands there, covering her gaping mouth with her hand. I wink at her.

I know I'm supposed to win this young man over for her, but I remember, too often, letting Ron Senior get away with little put-downs over the short while we were together. It didn't help. Keeping quiet and taking insults seemed to goad him into more. Maybe what he really wanted was more reaction from me. But I was busy with my two babies at the time. I didn't have time for one more big baby.

Hardeep smiles at me. Perhaps he's not as confident as Chael, but he has long eyelashes that curl up and around. Eyes that glow warm. "You look … um … nice today. Different somehow."

Chael climbs out of the pool, still with an angry glow. "Hey! Kick him into the pool, too. He's commenting on your body."

I lean toward Hardeep and place my hands on his young chest, pretending to go along with Chael's demand. I can feel his heart beating quicker. It's been so long since I've had this power over a young man. I give him a gentle push, and he laughs, taking a couple of steps back toward the pool. Then he just jumps sideways. Falling for me. Showing off for me.

I laugh, too. Flirting, such fun! Something I also haven't done for a long time.

When I turn to Chael, I notice a change in him, something subtle. His mouth straightens and his eyes darken.

Hallie walks over to me. "Should we work on our project after swimming's done?"

"What about the people you drove here?" I know Margret never likes any changes in her plans.

"They will have to wait. Linda already has a good book to read."

She's right, to heck with Margret. "Meet you in the library, then."

"Snack time for me. Second pass at the buffet! Ta-ta." Hallie gives me a wave.

The potluck, of course. I'd forgotten. I'm dying to join her. Wrong word; *dying*, that is. The camaraderie at these events actually makes me feel more alive, like we're all growing old together, like it's one big party. Barring that accident in the parking lot yesterday, I would have brought my specialty: Conferri Salad, made with orzo, various colours of peppers, and goat cheese. Will Gordon bring his spinach salad? I love the dressing he makes. If I live my life as Hallie from here on in, I will only date men who can make a good salad. I should ask Chael if he can cook; at the very least, he should be good with greens, named after a vegetable as he is.

As more young people drift into the pool area, the music is turned up louder. "Don't you dare step on my blue suede shoes." The Elvis hit seems to summon blue-haired Abby. Angel eyes grins a hello at me. "Cannonball anyone?" she asks and heads for the diving board.

Well, why not? I think and rush after her. The pool area echoes with laughter, yelling, and splashing that sounds like shattering glass. I love the power I feel as I leap off the board, bending my knees tight to my body. When I crash in, I send water all over Chael and Hardeep as well as the other teens in the pool.

The waterslide opens and I find I can climb up those stairs like nobody's business. I fly down, round and round. *Whee! Splash!*

I can't help smiling. I did not have *this* much fun at the pool last time I was this age. Youth really is wasted on the young.

When the next song begins, we all jump into the pool and dance. I twist to Chubby Checker, pony to the Beatles, and do the swim to Bobbie Freeman — all dances from my sock hop day, but so deliciously retro for these kids that they point at me and call "Cool!"

As "Love Me Tender" plays, Chael approaches to dance close with me in the water. No Kendra in sight. One person I did not invite. I try to keep some water space between us, but he draws closer.

I don't pull away. Hallie wants this boy and I want to give her back something for the loan of this lovely body — besides expensive cellphones and lunches and wild rides in my Hurricane, that is.

His hands reach for me and then take hold of my chin. For a moment he just smiles as his eyes lock onto mine.

If only he knew how old I really was.

Then he tilts his head and slowly leans in. Closer, closer, finally our lips touch, oh so softly. A whisper of velvet. Surprisingly, I find mine tingle.

As his lips linger, my face and body warm to an intense heat. I'm waiting for his lips to part. My own mouth loosens. The cool water surrounding us multiplies the tingling and the heat.

But then he pulls away.

And my body collapses in a sigh. This is all too wonderful.

Inside, I always felt like a teenager despite the way my body betrayed me.

But now it is glorious to look as young as I feel. Chael may be a boor but he's a good kisser.

After the 60s Swing and Swim ends, I change back into my street clothes and step out into the hallway. Abby needs to head home to babysit her kid sister, but Chael and Hardeep wait.

Hallie, in her eighty-two-year-old skin, waves to me from the other end, near the library.

I wave back and walk toward her.

"What's up with the old lady? Do you know her?" Chael asks as he and Hardeep tag alongside me.

"She's my grandmother," I answer.

"Yeah, sure. Wrong colour."

"Don't be an ignoramus!" I dig my fists into my hips. "Susan MacMillan is my adoptive grandmother for an empathy project. I'm going to get my volunteer hours helping her with technology. Come and meet her."

"That's okay. I have to floss my teeth. Let's go, Hardeep."

Ignoramus and a boor!

"You go ahead. My teeth are good." Hardeep smiles slowly, and they are … beautiful, nothing green stuck between them. "I want to meet Mrs. MacMillan."

"She might have friends who need help with their technology, too," I say, hoping to get Chael to stay, if only for the school credit. "You could put your volunteer hours in, too." I want Hallie to see him as he truly is. If she still likes him afterwards, then it will be her loss.

"Thanks anyway," he answers. As it turns out, he doesn't make his exit quick enough.

Hallie draws closer and I can see the way she's looking at him, like a hopeful puppy. In her current state — more like a hopeful old dog. I try to signal her with lifted eyebrows not to do that. She needs to remember what age her body is.

"Hi, Mrs. MacMillan. These are my friends Hardeep and Chael." I gesture toward them, and Hardeep holds out his hand and shakes hers.

Chael gives a wave and says, "Pleased to meet you and all that. But I gotta head off."

Hallie's mouth droops, but her eyes still follow him.

"I hear you and Hallie are working on a project together," Hardeep says cheerfully.

"Yes, and I want to show Mrs. MacMillan something on her El-Q. Do you have it here?" I ask.

"Yes, right in my purse." Hallie takes the device out.

Hardeep immediately leans over. "An El-Q! Cool! May I see it, Mrs. MacMillan?"

Hallie offers it to him and he takes it from her hand. "Wow. I wish my grandmother would get one of these. She won't go near a computer."

I feel myself blushing. I used to be that grandmother.

"Snail mail takes forever to India. It's like I don't even have grandparents. Does it take good photos?" he asks.

I shrug. "Try it."

"Okay. Squeeze in close for the selfie!" He holds up the device, his cheek touching my young face on one side and Hallie's wrinkled one on the other — it feels as though we are all magically linked together in this moment.

Click!

A perfect shot, all three of us captured looking happy. Even Hallie, in her eighty-two-year-old body, smiles.

He hands me back the phone. "I've heard it has a built-in stabilizer. Someone posted a video taken on a roller coaster ride and the image was crystal sharp."

A roller coaster. I catch Hallie's eye. "I want to show you the Saji Happy Motoring message board. Why don't we sit down?" We look around and find a table and chairs set up in front of the pool window. Everyone takes a seat. I continue. "A guy posted on the message board about sticking gas pedals. The same trouble you said you were having." The last sentence is for Hardeep's sake. He watches as I fumble to search for the site.

"Just go to your history," Hardeep suggests. He points to the button on the top line of my screen and I click.

I key in my username and password quickly. All my years of court stenography help — typing hasn't changed. Then I check the page. "Oh my! Even more people have posted." There's a Songbird, a Dogwalker, and an Applegirl all claiming to have issues. "Oh no! Applegirl had problems even after the throat plate was cleaned!" I turn my El-Q over to Hallie.

Hallie reads the messages on the El-Q.

Hardeep reads aloud from Hallie's side. "Applegirl thinks the gas pedal sticks if you hit the brakes hard and then step on the pedal."

I read over Hallie's other shoulder. Dogwalker also owns a Blizzard just like Ron. I look at Hallie. "Can you warn *your son*?" I can't help the emphasis I put on the last two words. My desperation. *My son, help my son, save him.*

"You know what he'll say. He knows how to drive," Hallie answers.

"Still. We have to at least try. Give him the opportunity to prepare. That little extra chance."

CHAPTER 17

Hallie

WELL, THIS IS AWKWARD. I WANT to warn Susan's son Ron that his Blizzard's gas pedal may stick but I don't know his phone number or have it in my contacts. Which I would if I were really Susan and not just a teen body snatcher. Fumbling for his contact info in front of Hardeep will look suspicious. Talking on a phone to this "son" I've only met once when we visited Sunnyside Terrace together will also be strange.

So I reason out loud for Hardeep's sake. "Um, I can't call Ron at work. He might be in the courtroom. I'll leave him a Facebook message. My Facebook account is new, too," I say as I type his name into the search box. A thumbnail photo of Ron MacMillan shows up. I click on it and find his page.

Immediately, I post a message to him, reading it out loud as I type: "Be careful with your gas pedal. A Blizzard owner had problems, too!"

"But how will you know that he gets it?" Susan asks.

I try to signal her with my eyes. Hardeep may think "Hallie" is a little too interested in a senior's business. I add, "Call me when you get this message," and give him the El-Q number.

Susan frowns but I can't think of what else to do to make her happy.

One of the lifeguards comes to our rescue now. "Hey, if you guys are hungry, there's a ton of food left over from the senior's potluck."

Susan and Hardeep look at each other. What kind of look is *that*? Her mood changed pretty quick. She's smiling. *What?* She can't possibly like him. She's way too old for him, at least on the inside.

Susan answers the lifeguard. "I'm starving."

She must have my appetite now. I'm not even worried that she'll overeat and make me gain weight anymore. *Eli, if you just give me my body back in time for Christmas, I promise I'll never complain about my thunder thighs again.*

"How 'bout you, Hardeep?" I ask. Back in my regular fifteen-year-old body, I know I wouldn't have wanted to hang around with any seniors. Just yesterday, on that bus ride to the mall, I hated being stuffed in there with all the old people. Eli especially.

"Free food. I'm in!" Hardeep answers.

The lifeguard points down the hall. "Just around the corner over in the party room. Tell everyone I sent you."

While I need to be alone with Susan at some point, it's nice to hang with one of my friends, even if it is only Hardeep.

"I'll take them over, if you like," I volunteer. Susan and I need to get to know each other better to cope with this switch.

"That would be great," the lifeguard answers.

Of course, I've left crabby old Margret in the glum, windowless party room, sitting and waiting. From an old boom box propped in the corner, an Elvis sound-alike croons, "Rudolph, the red-nosed reindeer."

By now, the banquet table groans with bowls of pasta, potato, and green salads, a creamy pink gelatin fish, a plate of cheese and crackers, grapes, strawberries, pickles, olives, and little round white onions. Another table has been added for the brownies, Nanaimo bars, and assorted shortbreads. Two large metal coffee machines sit there, one labelled apple cider. Too much food, as that lifeguard said.

Still, Margret jumps up and complains. "You young people didn't bring anything to this buffet, why should you be able to eat from it?"

"The staff invited us," Susan answers with my teen voice. "They didn't want the food to go to waste." She reaches out to shake Margret's hand, which confuses Margret for a moment. "Nice to meet you. Susan's told us so much about you."

That leaves Margret sputtering. It would be hard to think of anything nice to say about her.

"That goes for me as well, Mrs. ...?" Hardeep tilts his head and smiles.

"Kramer," Margret answers. She then makes an abrupt switch and turns almost nice. "You'll want to try Gordon's spinach salad. It's the bomb."

The bomb? Really? I lean toward Susan and talk softly into her ear. "Can I eat shortbread? Margret said it was bad for your gall bladder."

"Of course. She just likes to stuff them all in her face," Susan whispers back.

So I grab a cup of warm apple cider and pile a small plate with shortbread.

Susan fills her plate with spinach salad, some squares of orange cheese, a few slices of ham, and about five table-spoons of something white and orange. "Ambrosia," she tells Hardeep. "They glue marshmallows and mandarins together with mayonnaise."

"Vegetarian, though, right?"

She nods. "And surprisingly tasty."

He takes some.

The jolly Santa senior brings in some more kids who we don't know, and they grab some red paper plates and start serving themselves.

"Great salad, Gord," Susan calls out, forgetting her-self. If she's me, there's no way she would know this dude's name.

"Show some respect," Margret hisses and gives her the instant stink eye. "You don't address your elders by their first name."

Meanwhile, Gord plays air guitar as he skips around the table to the "Jingle Bell Hop."

"Sorry, I don't know your last name," Susan recovers as he pauses near us for a moment. "My adoptive grand-mother told me your salad is the best. And it is."

"Never mind." He smiles and pats the left side of his chest. "A young girl calling my name makes my heart skip a beat." He points to the metal bowl. "Candied pecans, that's the trick."

He's a sweet old guy and he reminds me of my Uncle Bill. He joins us at the table on the metal chair next to me, and we end up showing him as well as Margret how to use El-Q Hangout by contacting Susan's granddaughter Leah in B.C.

Susan squeals when Leah appears on the screen and I elbow her to warn her about blowing our cover. I have to pretend to be her, after all, to match the body I'm in.

"Hello, hello, Leah! We've heard so much about you," Gord calls and waves. Then he excuses himself, pulling Margret away with him to get coffee.

Hardeep stands. "Do you want to come with me to get some more shortbread?"

He's wanting Susan to leave with him to give me privacy with Leah, my supposed granddaughter.

"That's all right," I tell them. "Hallie better stay in case I press a wrong button."

"Bye, Leah!" He waves and leaves.

Susan leans over immediately and whispers in my ear. "Ask Leah if she liked the scarf and hat that I bought her. I never got a thank-you note."

Instead, I tell her, "Leah, I have a new Gmail account. I'll send you the address. I'm also on Facebook now."

Susan nudges me, all the while waving at the screen.

"Hang on," I grumble under my breath. "I'm getting to it." Facing the screen again, I introduce her. "This is my friend Hallie. She's teaching me all about the El-Q I bought." Then finally, "By the way, did you like the scarf and hat I sent you?"

"Yes, Nana. Did you knit them yourself?" The screen freezes her for a moment, mouth open, in crazy broken up pixels.

Susan whispers into my ear, "I bought them at the bazaar but don't tell her."

The mouth closes as the screen unfreezes again. I smile sweetly and answer, "Sure I did."

"Oh, then could you knit me a pair of matching mittens?"

I hesitate for a moment. Why would Susan want to pretend she knits, anyways? "Don't have any more of that colour wool." I gulp. For all I know, it's white.

Linda walks in then with her book tucked under her arm and clucks over the El-Q. I show her the screen and introduce her to my "granddaughter" Leah.

Leah and I chat a while about weather and Christmas. She wishes Susan could come out there this year.

"Tell her I miss her and that I love her." Susan's voice sounds low and husky in my ear.

I turn to Susan and see tears in her eyes. It must suck to have her real granddaughter live so far away. I turn back to the screen. "Okay, well we can talk again soon. On Christmas, for sure. I miss you." I pause for a moment. "I love you."

"I love you too, Nana." She waves.

There's an electronic *Ow* and the window closes. We're quiet for a moment.

Then Hardeep comes back and offers reindeer cookies all around. Gordon hands me a coffee. Margret asks, "Can I get hold of my daughter? She lives in Germany."

"Sure," Hardeep answers. "If you have an El-Q or computer, we can set you up with an account.

"You can borrow mine," I say. I can't imagine how I'd feel if my family lived on another continent. Would it feel like you just didn't have any kids anymore?

Margret frowns at her watch. "They're ahead of us by six hours. It's too late today."

"What about borrowing an e-reader from the library? Could you help me get books on it?" Linda asks.

"Sure can," Hardeep says.

We toss our paper plates into the garbage and then head back to the library. The seniors seem so excited about going electronic and it's such an easy thing to help them — I wonder why we've never done it before.

While they're busy, the El-Q burps and I step away from them all to answer. It's Ron.

"Hi, Mom. I got your message. Listen, we need to talk. Why don't I come over to the condo?"

"I'm not checking into that residence, no matter what."

"Whatever you say, Mom. I'll be there in a half an hour." *Click!*

Bossy, much? I put the El-Q back in Susan's purse. "Listen, we have to go now," I tell everyone. "My son's visiting me."

CHAPTER 18

Susan

IF THERE'S ONE THING I KNOW about my son, it's that he's prompt and expects everyone else to be, too. Hallie cannot possibly make it back to the condo within his appointed thirty minutes, especially since she has generously offered to drive everyone home. Perhaps she wants the companionship; being alone in another person's body is rather frightening, I find. Still, if everyone accepts the lift, she will be late.

Since I would actually like to see Ron, I make Hallie a counter-offer. "Why don't you just let us off at your building? You're right across from the mall. We can browse the stores and catch a bus from there, easily."

"That makes perfect sense," Margret agrees as she commandeers the front passenger seat. "We don't want to drive all over Burlington after all. We have things to do."

"I don't mind. Driving all over, I mean." Linda climbs in the back with Hardeep and me. "Be nice to take a little tour and I don't have anything else on my schedule for the rest of the day."

"The mall would be great," Hardeep chimes in and smiles at me.

I wink back, feeling a little wicked for doing so.

"All right. Buckle up," Hallie calls back to us.

We drive off ever so slowly.

I watch and see that Hallie keeps a consistent, even pressure on the gas pedal, no jerking us to a start or a stop. When she approaches the red light, the Hurricane slows down even more. I can't see what Hallie's doing with the accelerator, but I imagine she's avoiding it as much as possible. Cautious. Good for her. The car coasts to a stop, and Hallie flings her arm up suddenly, pointing to the snow-covered island in the centre of the road. "What is that?"

Hardeep cranes his neck. "Strangest-looking animal I've ever seen."

Margret leans forward, squinting. "A pig, I think. Did it fall off a truck?"

I squint in that direction, too. The creature is small, pink, and spotted, with a black tuft of hair on its head and tail and on each paw.

"Why, it's a dog," Linda says. "One of those hairless kinds. It must be freezing."

"Chinese Crested." I snap my fingers as I instantly recall the name of the breed. "It can't possibly make it across safely." Before anyone can try to change my mind, I fling open the door. "I'm going to help it."

Margret grumbles a warning about rabies in stray animals, but I jump out, anyway.

Hardeep follows.

Not foaming at the mouth, the small, naked dog flips on its back to offer me its belly, and I notice that it is a he. Large, brown eyes look up at me through the tuft of hair. His tail plume flaps at me.

"No collar." Hardeep frowns. "He's doesn't seem hurt, though."

"No. No cuts or bruises. He's friendly enough." I give his belly a little rub, and then before he can make a break for it, I scoop him up. Carefully, I cross back to the Hurricane, Hardeep at my elbow. He opens the car door for me.

"What are you going to do with a dog?" Hallie calls over her shoulder. "Your mother won't let you keep it."

And of course, she would know.

"Too bad. He's a cute little fellow in an odd sort of way." I always wanted a pet; Ron Junior was allergic, though. Would he have been all right around this breed? I slide into the back seat with the dog. He adjusts himself on my lap, sitting up and panting in a half-grin. I scratch at the tuft on the animal's head. He seems content.

"We can take it to the animal shelter," Hallie says, and eyes me from the rear-view mirror.

"But you'll be late for your son!" I argue. Ron will pace at the condo, checking his watch every few moments. He'll wonder why his dear old mother can't be punctual, since she's retired and work is the only commitment he understands. He will scold.

"It's the only thing to do, really," Margret pronounces. "We don't know if his owner is missing him, after all." For once, she seems agreeable, even if it does cause a kink in her busy schedule.

Hallie passes her El-Q over her shoulder to me. "Text Ron for me?" Meanwhile, she starts the car and slowly moves it forward.

As I grab the El-Q, the dog nuzzles my hand for more patting. "Just a moment, puppy." With the dog licking me now, I struggle to type: *Rescuing a dog, will be late.* I press send. Ron will assume I've gone doddery. He never much understands my love for pets. The dog calms back down when I pass the El-Q over to Margret in the front seat to put back in my old purse. "Do you know where the shelter is?" I ask Hallie.

"Um, no," Hallie answers.

"Just turn down Guelph, then off on Mountainside and down Industrial."

"Is that the street with all the auto-repair shops on it?" Hallie asks.

"Yes."

"What's the matter with you?" Margret grumbles. "A young girl knows the area better than you."

I quickly lie to cover up my unusual knowledge. "My dad took me along once to get his car repaired, and we visited the animal shelter while we waited."

Hardeep seems not to take notice of our geographical exchange at all.

He seems more bewildered by the dog. "I wonder how a Chinese Crested ended up on the street all by itself," he says.

"No collar, either, and no coat. Must be cold." I lean down to hug him warm but notice that, oddly, he does not shiver.

Hallie makes a slow turn on Guelph and a car honks from behind us. That car speeds around us.

"Never mind, it's good you're driving slow if we can't trust that gas pedal." I reach to pat her shoulder, then pull my hand away when I see Hardeep give me an odd look.

We hit another light and then turn onto Mountainside.

Suddenly, the dog paws at my cheek as if to push me away. "Ow, ow, stop!" His long, black nails scrape at my face till I brush off his paws. Still, they have forced me to turn toward the side window. Then I spot it. There at the Automagic Bodyshop, a tow truck sits with a red Hurricane attached to it. The front is crushed. What are the odds? I point and tell Hallie, "Look over there."

"That's a car just like yours. Same colour even," Hardeep comments. "Shame."

"I wonder how that accident happened," I muse out loud.

The dog gives a small sharp bark, *Rat!* like he wants to tell me something. This animal is too strange. It's as if he deliberately pushed me toward the window to notice that Hurricane. I look down at him and notice a dark blue line of squiggle above the crest of fur on his paw. I lift the paw closer to me and see the squiggle is actually writing. "Well, will you look at that; this dog has a tattoo."

"What does it say?" Hardeep asks, leaning close to me to see. "Any hint to where he belongs?"

"Carpe Diem." I read the words out loud for Hallie's sake. Then I lift my eyes to the rear-view mirror where the reflection of Hallie's eyes meets my own.

CHAPTER 19

Hallie

PULLING INTO THE EMPTY LOT of the Burlington Animal Shelter and parking is easy-peasy, which is great 'cause I'm not sure I trust the park assist feature on the Hurricane anymore. I turn to Susan and nod my head toward the door. "Can I speak to you for a second?" Then I turn to Margret. "You guys can just go on ahead."

Susan jumps out, with Eli, in the form of a Chinese Crested, tucked in her arms. Meanwhile, I rub the circulation back into my knees, then straighten slowly and step out. Only my second day in this body, but it feels like a hundred years and I know there's no skipping and bounding for me. Linda and Hardeep exit on the other side, with Margret hanging back just a little, out of nosiness or lack of energy, who knows.

"We'll meet you in there," Susan calls, and Margret takes the hint, shuffling toward the entrance of the animal shelter.

It's nippy outside and I hug my elbows around my bony body to stay warm. When they're all out of hearing range, finally, I speak to Susan. "Seriously, what are we going to do here? We can't put God in a dog pound."

Susan smiles a great big grin that makes me envious of my old mouth and teeth. "Oh, I don't know." She rubs the long tuft on the top of his head hard. "It might be good for him to see how the other half lives. Right, boy?"

Rat, rat, rat! The dog wriggles in Susan's arms. *Rat, rat, rat!* Suddenly, he breaks loose, makes a spectacular leap, and runs into the road. A white delivery truck brakes sharply, fishtails on the snowy road, with its rear end sliding toward the small animal.

I hold my breath. The truck straightens out of its skid and then continues on. No thump, and yet, suddenly, no dog either. The Chinese Crested has disappeared.

But that tow truck complete with the Hurricane hooked to the back still sits there at the shop.

"Where did he go?" Susan asks.

"Who knows?" I shrug my shoulders. "But I'm guessing Eli must want us to investigate that smashed-up Hurricane. Let's cross the street and see what we can find out."

The first thing I do is take pictures of the Hurricane with the El-Q, making sure to get the licence plate in my shot. Then we go inside the shop. A chime sounds as the door closes behind us, and the smell of oil and paint wafts in from the garage behind the counter. On the wall, a calendar with a St. Bernard chewing on an ornament reminds customers that the shop is closed on December 25. Four days away. I swallow hard. Christmas.

Happy holiday greeting cards surround it. How happy will it be as an eighty-two-year-old? I have to escape this body.

"Can I help you?" A guy in a blue shirt and dark pants steps in from the garage. His eyes are startlingly light blue, contrasting nicely with his dark hair and thick moustache. Cute for an old guy — only now he's a young guy compared to the body I'm stuck in.

"Can you tell us what happened to that car on the tow truck?" Susan asks.

"And its owner," I add.

"Sure. She went through a red light and a tractor-trailer plowed into her. The driver is in the hospital."

"Do you know which hospital?" Susan asks.

"Gee, no."

"Can you give us her name?" I ask.

"I'm not comfortable doing that, no. That's confidential."

"What if you give her our name and ask her to call us?" I ask.

"I guess I could do that if ..." He frowns.

"Tell her I'm a Hurricane owner, too, and I think there might be some defect in the gas pedal." I take out a piece of paper from the purse I carry, write down Susan's name, email, and cellphone number on it, and pass it to him.

He stares at it. "Listen, I'll definitely give it to her if I can ... it's just, well ... she may not make it."

"Oh," Susan says. Her green eyes fill instantly. Is she worried about her son or is she just an emotional old lady?

I grab her elbow and drag her to the door before she does or says anything weird that I won't be able to explain. "Thank you," I call back to the mechanic. The door chimes on our way out.

"Hey, what are you doing over there?" Margret calls from across the street. "Where is the dog?"

"He ran away. We chased him over here, but he disappeared," I answer as we walk back to the animal shelter.

"Shouldn't we look for him?" Hardeep asks.

"No," Susan snaps. "We did our best. He took off on us."

She's annoyed with Eli. Who can blame her? He's like the guy who videos an accident for YouTube but doesn't do anything to prevent it.

Hardeep looks confused but follows her to the car.

Margret mumbles something about being irresponsible. What would she say if she knew who the dog really was?

Back in the Hurricane with everyone buckled in, I start up and very carefully give it gas. No double taps or sharp braking. We will not crash while I'm driving. I slow down well before a light changes, just in case. Maybe Eli wanted to show us that red Hurricane as an additional warning. But couldn't he have just stopped the accident entirely instead?

Traffic crawls as people leave work. The sky turns inky black but the snow reflects back the street lamps. A cosy winter wonderland. As we roll into the condominium parking lot, I can see Ron as a dark silhouette against the bright light, standing in the entranceway, arms crossed.

I continue into the underground garage and pull into Susan's spot. No one's going to give me a lecture on parking in the visitor lot today. We walk to the elevator, Susan presses the button, and the doors open with a soft click. She presses Lobby, and in a moment, we face Ron.

"Where were you? I was so worried," he says by way of hello.

Susan wants to answer so I quickly cut her off. "Didn't you get my text? We went to the animal shelter."

"That's another thing. Since when do you text? I thought someone had kidnapped you and assumed your identity."

"Ron, meet Hallie, my technology coach," I say. "She's teaching me how to use my new El-Q. I'm her empathy project for school. Her adoptive grandmother."

Susan holds out her hand to shake Ron's. Her green eyes shine. Happy, proud? Hard to know.

"This is Hardeep, her friend, and you remember Margret and Linda?" I'm guessing he knows them, anyway. Hoping at this point.

"Darndest thing," Margret tells him. "We found one of those expensive bald dogs in the middle of the street."

Linda continues, "We couldn't just leave it there. It would have frozen."

"But then, your mother let it get away when we got to the animal shelter," Margret complains.

"For once, she did the smart thing. You don't want to fight with a stray." Ron defends me, all the while staring at me as though he wants to see what's inside my head.

"Well, I guess we'll be off," Hardeep says, breaking off an awkward moment. "Nice meeting you, Mrs. MacMillan," he tells me.

"Nice meeting you." What a sweet guy! But why couldn't Chael have hung out with us, too? "You catching the number four?" I ask Susan to let her know what bus she should take. Does that sound suspicious?

"The four, yes." Susan stays back a moment, just watching Ron, her eyes soft. "Take care of yourself," she says, and finally walks off with Hardeep.

"She's a sensitive girl, isn't she?" Linda says.

"Touched, if you ask me," Margret grumbles as she pushes the button on the side of the elevator door.

"Are you sure she doesn't want to sell you something?" Ron asks. "Has she asked for money?"

"No," I answer. "And I haven't given her any banking information."

The elevator chimes and opens for us, and, one by one, we step in.

"The teenagers need to earn volunteer credits to graduate," Margret explains.

"I think it's a lovely idea. Hallie and Hardeep seem like very nice young people," Linda says.

The elevator stops at the ninth floor and we all get off. "See you tomorrow," Margret says.

"Bye." Linda waves.

Ron and I walk toward Susan's condo. I fumble a little with her keys and feel Ron measuring me for that room at Sunnyside. The door unlocks and I push it open.

Ron steps in and heads to the washroom. I flop down on the couch. Ow, that hurts — I'll have to be more careful when I sit, too. I rub my hip bones.

The toilet flushes and I hear the taps, then, "Mom, are you not feeling well?"

"Well, my joints ache, but other than that, for an eighty-two-year-old, I'm doing okay. Why?"

"You didn't make your bed. There are clothes all over the floor." He walks to the living room via the galley kitchen and dining room. Checking on me? "You didn't clear the table." He squints at me, sprawled on the couch, and frowns. "Aren't you making us coffee?"

Gahhh! I don't know how to make coffee. "I'm off caffeine if you must know. Ron, please sit down for a minute. I have to show you something."

"What is it, Mom?" He stands there, arms folded across his chest. "Oh, your new toy. That's a little weird, too. You go from no cellphone to the most expensive El-Q model."

"I thought top-of-the-line would be more user-friendly." I smile at him apologetically. I hate that he puts me in a position where I feel like I'm guilty of something.

"User-friendly?" Ron tilts his head.

"Hallie's teaching me a whole new vocab. Great, right?" I pat the couch space beside me. "Here, sit."

Finally, he plunks down heavily.

I press and hold the button on the El-Q so I can use Genie. "Call up Saji Happy Motoring Club website," I tell her, concentrating on the screen for a moment. Once the site comes up, I check the message board. "It's about your car. Just a second. Here we are. There are all these people complaining about accelerator problems ... Well, that's odd."

"What's odd, Mom? The fact that you talk to your phone now?" He's shaking his head.

"No, they're not here anymore." I scroll up and then back down. Sport's and Crazypants's complaints are still up.

"Who's not there anymore?" Ron doesn't even look at my screen.

"Hotrod, Songbird, Dogwalker, Applegirl … all of them are gone." I move the El-Q so he's forced to look at it.

He glances down, and then back up at me. "What are you talking about?"

"The people who complained about their accelerator sticking."

He shrugs his shoulders. "What does that matter?"

"Don't you understand? Saji Motors has a big problem with their gas pedals. And it's not just in the Hurricane. Hotrod said his Blizzard's accelerator still sticks."

"Well, I've never experienced any problems."

"Not yet, you haven't. The comments have all been taken down. Don't you think that's weird? It's like Saji Motors is deliberately hiding the problem."

"Mom, I'm starting to think a lot of things are weird."

"What, because I'm a slob — um — a little untidy today?"

"No. There's something else we need to discuss. Can you put that thing away for a second?"

I close the window and place the El-Q on the coffee table.

"Thank you. I called the police station today over your speeding ticket. But Officer Wilson had already forwarded it to the traffic prosecutor."

"So?"

"I spoke to the prosecutor, and there's a recommendation for you to have your driving skills reassessed.

Officer Wilson reported that you seemed to be highly confused. That you relied on your granddaughter to find your driver's licence."

"Oh crap!"

Ron pulls back. "*Oh crap?* Mom!" He shakes his head. "Seriously, you are eighty-two years old. You're entitled to be confused. You should also be able to put your feet up and have other people shop and cook and clean for you."

"You want me to move into that home with bland food and unclean seniors."

"They have baths twice a week, they're not 'unclean.' Besides, it doesn't have to be that one."

"I don't want to die."

"Of course not" — he reaches around my shoulders and hugs me — "nobody wants that."

"But living in Sunshine Terrace is just slow dying." I lean away.

"You don't know that till you try. They have lots of activities. They would bus you to Aquafit."

"I want to do things for myself. I want to live until I die. Do you understand me?" I'm sputtering, I'm so angry for Susan.

"Yes, Mom, I do. But do you understand me? With a reckless driving charge and possible licence suspension, no one's going to buy your Saji Motors conspiracy theory. Once you go to court, you won't be driving yourself again."

CHAPTER 20

Susan

I LOVE BEING YOUNG AGAIN! I step out of the condo building, inhale the cold air, and let it out in a slow, smoky cloud. I love the way Hardeep looks at me.

"Can I ask you something?" he says.

"Certainly." Diamonds twinkle in the sky behind his head.

Hardeep tentatively takes my hand. "I like you." He pauses.

"I like you too," I answer. "But that's not a question." Can I afford to forget that I am really eighty-two years old? Just for a moment can I enjoy the sensation of his warm fingers curled around mine?

He grins. "I'd like to go out with you … only, how do you feel about Chael? I mean, he kissed you …"

He isn't worth the time of day. That's what my mother said about Ron Senior when I first brought him home, and Mom was right. Some small part inside me knew it even then, but it didn't stop me. And it won't stop the real Hallie from falling in love with the boy less worthy, either. I don't want to play coy with Hardeep, but I can't hurt his feelings. "I'm not sure," I answer finally. "Can we keep it friendly for a while and see?"

His smile drops.

This kind of answer would have made Ron Senior rage and sulk. It will be a true test of Hardeep.

"Sure." His mouth straightens back up as he brightens again. "Do friends kiss?"

"Why not?" I ask, more of the universe than in answer to Hardeep — but this may be my last chance to be young and alive, after all.

Hardeep leans in and touches his lips to mine. So gentle, so sweet. He presses in for more, but I break away. A second kiss from someone less than a quarter of my soul's age. These are impossible feelings I'm having. Falling for this young boy.

"I don't want to go to the mall again, do you?" he asks.

"No. Do you want to just catch the bus?" The number four, I remember. But does Hardeep take the same one? Does Hardeep even live in the same neighbourhood?

"Yes, I should head home."

We stroll toward the bus shelter still holding hands. Suddenly, music burbles from my coat pocket.

"Sorry, my El-Q," I explain, taking it out. When we arrive and stop at the small Plexiglas hut, I thumb my way to the message.

It's Hallie, and her text reads, *Connecting from the bathroom. Complaints on Saji message board disappeared.*

"How can that happen?" I wonder out loud. Just to make sure, I visit the Saji Motors message board, but of course, Hallie's right. "All the gas pedal posts are miss-ing." I turn to Hardeep.

He looks over my shoulder. "That's crazy. Usually someone approves comments before they go up. Why would someone take them down after?"

The El-Q burbles again. I flip to the messages. *Ron says police recommended court take away your driving licence.*

"Oh no!" I cry out. "We need to contact those people on that message board. Susan's going to lose her licence."

"Well, she is eighty-two, after all," Hardeep says.

"And you're a male teenager. They don't like you driving, either. Susan doesn't deserve this. The speeding wasn't her fault."

"You're right. Susan does seem like a super-careful driver." He knits his brows for a moment. "Maybe we can find the people who complained on Twitter or Tumblr."

"How? They use nicknames."

"I dunno. Some people use the same aliases for all their social media."

"Hotrod, Songbird, Dogwalker, and Applegirl," I recite, amazed again at my teen brain's excellent memory.

The bus rumbles in the distance.

"I can search for them if you like when I get home," Hardeep suggests.

The bus rolls alongside of us now and squeals to a halt.

I have to think quickly. I want to look for those peo-ple myself, but who knows if my newly acquired technol-ogy skills are up to it. "Why don't you come to my house? We'll do it together."

"Sure." He smiles.

A *sish* and a gust of warm diesel air, and the bus door opens for us. I slip the El-Q in my coat pocket and board, with Hardeep following.

I select a double seat in the middle of the bus and slide to the window. Hardeep sits down beside me, close enough so that our upper arms brush against each other. With our heavy coat sleeves between us, I can't feel his warmth. Still, the closeness feels comfortable, protective even. How can the real Hallie not fall for this young man, so sweet and considerate. I smile as I imagine a whole new do-over life where I choose the right person to be with instead of the "bad boy."

The bus takes us slowly through an industrial park. For a few minutes, the window acts as a framed piece of darkness, but I turn toward Hardeep and ignore the inky square. It's like turning away from death and paying attention to youth and energy and maybe even love. What if I stay in this body till it grows old? Can I live one more life? Have a relationship with this attractive young man? I can't believe I'm even considering it.

The bus veers into a housing development and Christmas lights pulse. I find myself leaning back on Hardeep and marvelling: coloured teardrops and white icicles alike. Gold and silver reindeer graze on the snow.

In the daylight, I hadn't paid much attention to all these decorations, but the darkness showcases the display.

A panicky thought suddenly bubbles up through the glow. What kind of lights hang from Hallie's eaves-troughs? I feel too hot. The smell of wet wool tickles my nose and the back of my throat. Everything looks so different at night, I won't recognize what's supposed to be my home.

But Hardeep solves that problem by leaping up and yanking at the signal rope. "Your stop, my lady." He sweeps his hand out to guide me.

My hero. "You know where I live." Thank goodness, since I don't. I sigh with relief and stand up.

He grins openly. "I saw you walking with Abby one day and followed you. I've liked you for a long time."

Some might consider such behaviour to be stalking — if it were someone repellent to them especially. But I think his dedication is romantic. I shuffle behind Hardeep, down the aisle, and step off the bus through the accordion-pleat door.

Hardeep continues to lead the way. I wonder if he hasn't come by Hallie's house again to pine over her. In her front yard, there's a little inflated carousel where a snowman, a reindeer, and a candy cane circle to the tune of "Frosty the Snowman." How could I have missed that? I will have to train myself to be more observant.

I catch myself reaching for the doorbell and just in time drop my hand to the doorknob. Turns out the door is unlocked. We walk in and hang up our coats in the closet. "Mom!" I call. "Aria?" No answer. "Dad?"

"If you have a computer, we can divide the list and search faster," Hardeep says.

"Yes. A computer. In the basement, I think. Sorry, my dad has been moving furniture around," I lie. "I'm going to the bathroom. You go on ahead." I open the door to the stairs for him and then rush around the ground floor, looking in rooms for computers, just in case.

Nothing. It has to be downstairs. I head toward the basement myself.

"What's your password?" Hardeep calls.

I freeze. I don't know all the family birth dates, which is how I made up my own bank pin number. I've heard people use pet names, but the Princes don't own an animal. Quickly, I message Hallie. *Urgent, need computer password. Hurry.* I call back to Hardeep, "I don't know. It's usually already on when I use it."

The El-Q burbles and I read Hallie's answer. *Prince123.* I call it out as I continue down the stairs.

"Turns out Songbird is a recording studio and a singer," Hardeep says as I approach.

"Well, you can be a singer and still drive a Hurricane. Why don't you email her?" I make it to the little alcove where Hardeep's voice is coming from and pull up a chair beside him. Close to him like this, I want to trace my fingers over his lips.

"What should I say?"

Can I live this life? I wonder again. "Ask if she drives a Saji car and whether she's ever had problems with the accelerator."

"Okay. I'll sign it with your name since this is your account."

"Certainly." I want to pull his cap from his head and run my fingers through his hair. Instead, I take out my El-Q. "I'll look for Applegirl." I type the word in the search window, and moments later, I'm overwhelmed with what Hardeep calls "hits."

"Better try quotation marks around the whole word,"

Hardeep says. "*Dogwalker* has too many matches even with them."

I lean in closer to Hardeep, then pull back. I add quotation marks around *Applegirl* and search again.

"I'm going to add *Burlington* to *Dogwalker* to cut down on some of the hits." He types at the computer for a bit, and I find I just want to sit back and watch him.

"But the person who complained could have been from anywhere in North America, really." I lean closer again.

"No, I think the Saji site is the local dealer's." Hardeep frowns. "Still, there are a lot of dog walkers in Burlington, too. I mean, do we really want to email all of them?" He turns to look at me. His lips turn up, his eyes catch fire.

I feel my cheeks heat up, and I quickly glance down at the screen. "Wait a minute. I've got something here. On this blog, Applegirl talks about buying a Hurricane."

CHAPTER 21

Hallie

GUESS I SHOULD BE HAPPY HE hasn't brought Sheryl along, but man, this son of Susan is annoying. He's standing in front of what's supposed to be *my* fridge and browsing inside.

"You don't seem to have any groceries, Mom. What are you planning to eat tonight?"

None of your beeswax, I want to tell him. Seems like everything poor Susan does or doesn't do is open to Ron's prying eyes. Instead I think fast. I don't want to be the reason he forces Susan into a home. "We had a big potluck lunch at the community centre. I thought maybe I would skip supper."

"Aw, Mom, how will you take your medications then?"

"Maybe with a piece of toast?" I'm winging it here. Does Eli have any idea how hard this body switch is to manage?

"Listen, why don't I take you to Denninger's and buy you a schnitzel sandwich?"

Denninger's is the deli next door. I've seen it but never been. Not exactly a hot spot for anyone under forty but what can I say? "Okay, sure." The El-Q belches and Ron squints at me.

"Excuse me. Just let me go to the bathroom first." I dash to the can and sit on the john to check my message. Susan says she needs our computer password. I text it to her, then flush, wash my hands, and try to fix my makeup. What can I possibly do with this apple-doll face? I add a layer of liquid cover-up, which evens out the skin colour to a super-pale beige. Every wrinkle turns into a ridge. How do people deal with skin like this, anyway? I brush some blush on my cheeks and end up looking like an old lady with a fever. Then I roll on some of Susan's favourite bright red lipstick. I grin. Scary! These teeth have seen brighter days. I step out.

"Did you remember to bring your pills?" Ron asks.

"I would have in a minute," I grumble, turning back to the washroom. I reach into the medicine cabinet for the rectangle of weekday boxes and pop Tuesday PM, dumping the pills in my hand. What to put them in till we eat? Maybe a zip-lock bag? I go to the kitchen and open and close drawers.

"What are you looking for?" Ron calls.

"A baggie for my pills."

He tromps into the kitchen, opens up a top cupboard, and pulls out a small empty vial. "Reduce, reuse, recycle." He frowns as he hands it to me. "And avoid plastic, it causes cancer."

"Indeed." That's what older people say, right? Instead of "whatever"? Am I blushing? I dump the pills in the vial and stick it in Susan's purse. "But I have to die of something."

Ron gives me a quick, sharp look.

Whoops! Said the wrong thing again. I grin and wink to soften the words and also to show him I'm not suicidal.

He chuckles. "True enough." He picks up my coat from the couch and holds it up by the shoulders to help me slide my arms in.

Coats on, we step out of the condo, and I lock the door behind us. We take the long walk to the end of the hall, ride the elevator to the lobby, and head outside. I can see Ron's Blizzard parked in one of the nearby visitor spots. "Should we walk?" he asks. "It's only a block, and by the time we find parking there …"

"Yes, let's." Really, I hate using these creaky skinny legs, but what if the accelerator sticks while we're driving?

Ron guides me by the elbow, and it takes about a half hour. In my regular body, I could have sprinted it in five minutes.

Everything in the deli is strange to me, and I know every move I make causes more eye-narrowing on Ron's part. Dining is cafeteria-style, so I slide a tray along and make stumbly slow decisions on questions the servers ask. Does Susan usually have sauerkraut with her schnitzel or not? Does she like fried onions on top or maybe some ketchup or mustard? In the end, I ask for them to hold everything and get it plain, ordering a decaf coffee to go with the sandwich. I dump in tons of milk and sugar.

"I just don't know what's come over you," Ron says as we sit down. "Everything you do seems so different. Maybe you had a stroke. Did you have a sudden strange headache, slurred words, blurred vision?"

I pat his hand, acting like some kind of television granny. "Changin' it up a little, sonny. At eighty-two years,

I should be able to do that — you said so yourself." I take a bite of my schnitzel sandwich. "Mmm, this is good."

He chews at a piece himself, then swallows. "Mom, I love you." He shakes his head as though he can't believe this line himself.

"Why does this not sound like a good thing?" I ask him.

He sips his coffee, delaying his answer, then looks up. "Because I just don't think you can live by yourself anymore."

"And if you didn't love me?"

"I just wouldn't bother you about it."

I let go a sigh. Being stuck in this aching aging body is the worst. Put this body in a home, and I know I'd have to kill myself to escape. I just can't hold out to see what crazy new ride Eli will put me on.

"Hear me out. Since your heart attack, every time the phone rings, Sheryl and I look at each other and freeze."

I frown and make up my mind to quiz Susan on this whole heart attack thing. "And you and Sheryl looking at each other, freezing, will help me in what way?"

He holds his forehead with his hand. "When you came late the other day, we worried you had fallen down somewhere. We don't want to go on holidays in case something happens to you. Sheryl is sick of staying home all the time."

"If something happens to me, it will happen whether you go away or not. You can look at each other and freeze in another country, for all I care."

"You're being selfish, Mom," he snaps. "If you lived at Sunnyside Terrace, we wouldn't have to worry all the time."

"You could forget about me."

"Yes … no. Well, maybe a little."

"Then pretend I'm in a home and forget me now," I tell Ron. "That way, I can just live my life."

"Sheryl can't just leave it alone." He sighs. "Work keeps me so busy I hardly have time to go on holidays, anyway." He pats my hand. "Don't forget to take your pills."

I close my eyes for a moment. I would have forgotten them. Then I open them again. "Thanks for reminding me." I take the vial out and swallow them with the coffee. Ugh. So many of them, and twice a day. "About Saji Motors," I say.

"That again?"

"Well, it's very important. You need to take this seriously and be very careful when you drive."

"I'm always careful. And I know how to drive in an emergency situation."

"Bully for you. Who's being selfish now?" I stare directly into his eyes. He has to look away. "What if a few people step forward and say they've had problems with their gas pedal?"

"You're going to dig up some drivers who've had trouble, right?"

I nod.

"Nobody's really going to pay much attention. Unless …"

"Unless what?"

"Unless someone has a major accident and you can prove it was the accelerator."

That Hurricane jacked up on the tow truck, the one the stupid dog-God made us notice. I whip out the El-Q and tap my way into photos and the picture I took of it. I hold the device in front of Ron's face. "The mechanic told us that the driver was in the hospital, in critical condition, by the sounds of it."

"And you know for a fact the accelerator caused the accident?"

Hmm. Why else would Eli force us to pick him up in the middle of the road and then leap in front of a truck to cross the street to an auto-body shop. He wanted to draw our attention to the crushed Hurricane, that's why. "Yes, I do."

"Can I ask what proof you have? Did the driver tell you this?"

My proof is a Chinese Crested dog who is really God. You could see where this wouldn't stand up well in a court of law.

"No, but she will when I find her." That is, of course, if I can find her and if she is still alive.

CHAPTER 22

Susan

THE EL-Q MAKES A STRANGE RINGING noise reminiscent of those black telephones of my youth — the ones with the long, curly wires. I have no idea what to do. How can I appease it?

Hardeep nudges me. "That's your El-Q, aren't you going to answer?"

"Oh, oh sure! Hello?" I hold the El-Q up to my ear like one of those receivers from my childhood.

"You're a riot, you know." Hardeep laughs. "Click the Hangout icon."

Icon, hmm. From Hallie's demonstration of the device in the IQ store, I know not to look for, say, Alice Munro's face. Instead, I scan the screen and notice a little green phone shaking; it has to be the icon. I tap it. Hallie's blue-haired friend, Abby, appears, grinning a glittery brace-toothed smile and waving. "Hey, foxy girl!" she squeals. "Can't believe hunky Chael kissed you! What was it like?"

"I can't talk about that now." I turn the El-Q so that Abby can see Hardeep. He pretends to be studying the computer screen. "I'm doing some research with Hardeep."

"Ohhhhh!" Abby takes a moment, then recovers. "Well, that sounds nerdy. For school?"

"No. It's a favour for Susan. We're trying to prove her car is defective."

"Susan? That old lady who knocked you down with her car? Why?"

"Because if she can't prove her gas pedal sticks, she'll lose her licence."

"I'd say that might be a good thing. Why does a hundred-year-old lady need to drive, anyway?"

"Well, she can't fly on her broomstick like you." A hundred years old, *harrumph*. I happen to know my other body looks in better shape than some of the seventy-year-olds hobbling around out there.

"*We* take the bus," says Abby. "So do lots of old folks, as you know. Isn't it dangerous when elderly ladies drive?"

"Not if they're good drivers. Research says seniors may have slower reflexes but they're still more cautious and that prevents accidents." I know I'm lecturing and that this wouldn't be like Hallie at all, but I don't care. I'm sick of everyone trying to yank away my last piece of independence.

"Okay. Well …" She switches gears. "I'm going to take Charlie to the dog park. I thought you might want to come." The screen suddenly changes angles and the head of a panting golden retriever fills the view. "High-five, Charlie!" Abby's voice calls from off-screen and a massive paw appears.

Hardeep looks over and smiles. "May as well go. Once you email Applegirl, there's not much else we can do … except wait."

"Right, certainly," I answer the dog paw on the screen, tapping my hand lightly against it.

Charlie gives a little yip.

The laptop switches angles again and Abby grins. "Great. We'll be there in five minutes."

Abby's image instantly disappears. I'm left with a tiny thumbnail photo of my young Hallie-self in the corner.

"Hang up," Hardeep suggests, then shuts down the internet on the home computer and stands up.

I click on the phone icon again, feeling like I'm conquering technology one keystroke at a time. Then I click contact on Applegirl's blog. Hardeep watches over my shoulder as I type on the blank, white form that appears.

> Dear Applegirl,
>
> You don't know me but my name is Hallie and my grandmother drives a Hurricane. Yesterday, the accelerator stuck on the QEW and we barely made it to the side of the road. She also got a ticket for speeding. We're looking for another driver who called herself Applegirl on the Saji message board. Her car's gas pedal sticks too. Are you that Applegirl?
>
> Yours truly,
> Hallie

"'Dear Applegirl'? 'Yours truly'? That sounds so snail mail," Hardeep says.

"I like snail mail — it's retro." With him, it's easy to bluff through my lapses in computer culture. I click send.

"I like everything you do," Hardeep says and leans close.

Then closer. I feel his warm breath on my skin and my young heart performs a double beat. I enjoy the sensation of his lips against mine, gentle and so sweet. But the doorbell rings and I force myself to pull away. Just as well — we can't fall in love. Surely to Eli, Hallie will return to her body at some point and will continue crushing on Chael. Hardeep and I both jump up at the same time and awkwardly head for the stairs together.

Ground floor again, in more ways than one. I let Abby and Charlie in as Hardeep and I get our coats.

Charlie wags patiently, his thick golden tail flapping against my legs. Hardeep holds Hallie's jacket up for me, something Ron Senior never did for me. Then we're both ready and out the door with Abby and the dog.

Hardeep reaches to hold my hand, but I swing my arm to avoid him. I don't want Abby to see these displays of affection; she doesn't seem like a great secret keeper. Luckily, Charlie takes up too much room on the sidewalk for the three of us to walk together so I allow Abby to lead the way.

Because, of course, I don't know where the dog park is. Around the next block, Hardeep begs off. "I'm expected home for dinner now," he says. "Let me know if Applegirl answers."

There's another awkward moment where we would've surely kissed if we were alone. Instead, he smiles and his eyes hold onto mine as he chucks me on the shoulder.

Now I move up alongside Abby. Charlie pulls hard ahead of us because he certainly knows and likes where we're heading. We duck through a catwalk, an ironic name for a path that leads to a dog park.

The park itself turns out to be a long, wide strip of field between two rows of houses. To one side, a few dog owners stand at a picnic table under a lamppost, sipping from paper coffee cups, steam rising white against the near dark. One woman flips through a newspaper, and I find myself longing to snatch it from her. I miss my morning reading habit so much. Instead, I check the row of cars parked nearby for a Saji Hurricane. Three different sport-utes but no Saji cars.

Abby unsnaps Charlie's leash and he breaks into a joyful gallop. A pack of four border collies chase a flying ball toward Charlie — the man throwing it must be a dog walker. Can we be that lucky? Really, what are the odds? Still, Eli enjoys playing tricks on us, so I try. "Excuse me. What kind of car do you drive?"

"Why?" The man grabs a drool-covered yellow tennis ball from one of the black-and-white dog's jaws and places it in a cup on the end of a blue plastic stick. "Did I leave my lights on?"

"No. I'm just looking for Dogwalker."

The man flicks the stick high in the air and the dogs hurl themselves after the ball again, Charlie joining in the fun. "Well, here, let me give you my card." He hands me a small rectangle of cardboard that reads *Noble Dog Walking* along with an email address and phone number.

"No, no. I don't own an animal. But I wanted to talk to someone who drives a Saji and calls themselves Dogwalker on message boards."

"Well, a bunch of us call ourselves that. And those cars are pretty popular, too."

"Yes." Darn. I knew finding the right Dogwalker couldn't be this easy. On the other side of the picnic table, Abby chats up a young handsome owner of a black standard poodle. My gaze drops to the woman sitting reading the newspaper. Just as she finishes, I can't help myself. "Do you mind?" I ask the woman, rushing to scoop it up.

"Knock yourself out."

An old habit, I flip to the obituaries, skimming them for any friends who may have died recently. I have outlived so many and often attend funerals where I reacquaint myself with some of the remaining few. That's when I see it.

> Suddenly, December 19. Sarah Ann Davidson, at age 19. Sarah leaves behind her mother Janet Grant and father Hugh Donald Davidson along with a brother Caleb and a sister Kiera. She will be sadly missed by the employees of Davidson Apple Orchards, where she worked in the marketing department. A life celebration will be held ...

A cold icicle runs down my spine. In obituaries, certain code words cue the reader as to the nature of the death. *Peacefully* is usually reserved for people who die of old age in a hospital or hospice bed. *After a long illness* or *a valiant battle with* indicates the obvious. Donations to whatever organization the family chooses usually tells you what disease their loved one died of. *Suddenly* usually signals some kind of accident, especially in a person so young. Did Sarah die in a car crash? The December 19 death date is a couple of days ago, a little early for that wreck on the tow truck. But maybe the body-shop mechanic didn't know she'd died. Sarah also worked for Davidson *Apple* Orchards.

So Eli didn't hand me Dogwalker but he probably led me to Applegirl, in which case I wouldn't be receiving an email back from her any time soon.

CHAPTER 23

Hallie

AFTER SUPPER MY BOSSY NEW SON makes me grocery shop with him. "You need to eat dairy, vegetables, and protein," he tells me as he loads up the cart with milk, bread, eggs, and some specialty cheese-and-spinach sausages. Wow, he really treats his mom like she's a baby. The sausage is his idea of a vegetable. "It will help keep you healthy. So you can live longer."

Does Susan even want to live longer? I grab a frozen pizza, a box of Frosted Flakes, and a strudel on the last leg toward the cashier, and Ron gets lots of eyebrow exercise from these choices. "This is so I will be happy while I'm alive," I explain, which you wouldn't think I would need to do, given that I, or at least Susan's credit card, will pay for these groceries.

Ron carries the bags back to my new condo, and before leaving, he gives me one more shot. "So we're agreed? I'm only going to approach the judge if you can find someone who has suffered an accident and can confirm it is as a result of a sticky gas pedal. I'm not going to fight for your licence over some imaginary problem that you can't prove is happening."

"You think this is all about me keeping my licence. Shouldn't Saji Motors be forced to repair car defects?"

He opens his hands wide. "Come to me with real facts and we can fight them on it."

"Fine, I will."

"And Sunnyside Terrace. You'll think about it?"

"I'll try ..." *not to*, I finish in my own head.

He sighs. "For me, this is all about keeping you safe. You're the one I care about."

It sounds like stuff my parents tell me when they say I can't go to late-night concerts or parties without parental supervision. ("I don't care about what all the other kids do. All I care about is you.") But Susan is eighty-two. Why does she need this? I can't help feeling bitter for her. "You want me safe, tucked in some home, away from heavy machinery and vehicles."

"Is that what it seems like to you?" He looks straight into my eyes, then looks away and shrugs. "You will be safer in Sunnyside."

"Yes, but will I be happy?"

He frowns. "You used to tell me all the time that wherever you go, whatever you do, you make your own happiness."

Really? Susan said this? "Yeah, well, Sunnyside would be a real challenge to that theory."

He smiles at that.

"Good night, Ron."

"Good night, Mom." He kisses my lips, a dry-lipped quick son-and-mother peck. Still. *Blah!*

If I don't get another chance to live my life in my

own body, his lips will be the only male ones to kiss mine besides my father's. I give him a grandmotherly hug — not too hard, don't want to hurt myself. "Goodbye, dear."

Then I go in, shut the door, and, as I look around, take a deep breath.

I better clean this condo — continued slobbiness may score me or Susan a bed at Sunnyside. First I put the groceries in the fridge and cupboard. Then I collect the coffee shop cups from the table and pitch them in the garbage pail under the sink. From there, I drift to Susan's bedroom, and even though it's almost time to go to bed again, I pull the sheets tight and tuck them in, smoothing the duvet over neatly. Finally, I pick up all the flowered blouses I threw around this morning in an attempt to dress non-florally and hang them back up in the cupboard.

By that time, I'm breathing hard and sweating from this light housework. When the El-Q goes off, I think, *Yay, saved by the burp*, and I'm happy to flop down on the couch and read Susan's text.

Applegirl may have been the driver of that Saji car on the tow truck.

I type back: *Really? Why do you think that?*

She answers: *A sudden death listed in the obits today. Sarah Davidson.*

How do you know Sarah's death was from that car accident? I answer.

Don't know for sure. Good date, mostly. No other cause of death listed, Sarah's young age. Obits would usually list heart attacks or cancer.

It sinks in suddenly. Oh my God, someone died because of the gas pedal defect! Someone else, that is. Although technically I haven't died because of the accelerator, at least not yet. Who knows what Eli will decide?

Why do you think Sarah is Applegirl? I text.

Obit says Sarah worked for Davidson Apple Orchards.

We have to find out for sure if it's her. We need proof, I answer.

We could go to the funeral. Tomorrow at 10. Smiths on Brant.

Ew, I think, then type: *First let me check what's on the internet about the accident.*

Susan replies, *OK Keep in touch.*

Immediately, I enter the words *car accident* along with the date in the search window. A bunch of articles pop up — people really should drive more carefully. So I take a leap and add the word *Hurricane* to narrow it down.

And there it is.

FATAL CRASH AT FAIRVIEW INTERSECTION

Police continue to investigate the fatal crash that occurred Saturday at the intersection of Fairview and Guelph and are asking for any witnesses to step forward.

Nineteen-year-old driver Sarah Davidson succumbed to injuries after her Hurricane ran a red light and collided with a tractor-trailer. The driver of the truck escaped with only minor injuries. Witnesses claim the Hurricane was travelling at high speed through the intersection and did not appear to brake.

Alcohol is not considered a factor. The popular marketing director of Davidson Apple Orchards had just finished delivering Christmas presents for the Santa Run and was headed to the mall to complete her shopping.

This could be the proof Ron needs! I text him the link.

It doesn't take long for him to answer. *A nineteen-year-old speeder dies running a red light. How does that prove the gas pedal stuck?*

I think about it for a moment — the way he mentions Sarah's age. Susan is too old and Sarah is too young, apparently, to be considered reliable drivers. Then I type. *Because she's the one who complained about her accelerator on the Saji message board.*

The alleged complaint that disappeared? he answers.

Yes, I type. If only I had kept a screenshot. This whole thing gets more depressing by the minute. I think for a moment. I don't want to go to Sarah's funeral, but somehow I need to get more information. Finally, I answer Ron: *I will get you your proof.*

Then I text Susan back. *All right, you win. We'll go to the funeral. I'll pick you up tomorrow at 9:30.*

CHAPTER 24

Susan

NEXT MORNING I SEARCH HALLIE'S cupboard for something suitable to wear to a funeral. It seems hopeless. Just how many pairs of jeans can one person own? And leggings, black leggings. Finally, I find a flowered black dress hidden at the back, with tags still on it. A bit summery, but paired with leggings and a sweater, it will have to do. Of course, for footwear, Hallie has nothing but sneakers scattered around the floor of her bedroom, and five pairs of flip-flops.

In my stocking feet, I grip the railing as I climb down the steps to the kitchen. Without shoes on, stairs can be so slippery. Hallie's mother sits at the table already, with an almost empty cup of coffee. I pour myself a cup and top off Mrs. Prince's. She actually startles and gasps.

"Sorry, uh, Mom, did I frighten you?"

Mrs. Prince squints. "Frighten? Um no, but you're in that dress Grandma got you. Let me take a picture to send her." She dashes out of the room and returns, raising her phone in front of her face. "Smile!" she calls.

And I do.

Click!

"One more!" And *click* again. Then, grinning as she looks at the tiny screen, Hallie's mother sits down again to her coffee.

In an attempt to be more Hallie-like, I grab the box of Frosted Flakes from the cupboard and pour myself a bowl. It's not as hideous as you might imagine. Crunchy, sweet, with that chaser of cold milk. I turn to Mrs. Prince. "Would you have any shoes I could borrow? To wear with this dress?"

"Hmm, maybe. But why don't you just wear the winter boots I bought you? There's snow on the ground and the boots are black. They'll go with your dress."

"Okay." I sigh. Pretending to be someone else is especially difficult in the morning. "I don't remember where they are."

"In the hall closet. Where else would they be? You haven't worn them once yet."

A clue! The boots are new and black. Hopefully, I can pick them out of the lineup. I sip at my coffee. *Ahhh.* Something warm to welcome the morning.

"So what's the big occasion? Doing something exciting today?" Mrs. Prince asks.

"Oh, just spending time with my project grandmother. Going to a funeral."

"What?" Hallie's mother sputters. "Really? Will you be all right?"

"What do you mean?" It's been so long since I had a mother, I forgot how concerned they can get.

"You've never been to a funeral before."

I shrug. I think that's a teenager thing to do. "But it isn't someone close." She has me worrying about Hallie now, though, because in reality, I've been to many funerals. My parents' and my sister's were the most difficult, but apart from the loss of the particular person who died, they can be quite pleasant. Relatives and old acquaintances you rarely see attend, there are usually photos or a video, memories revisited, and often a lovely reception or at least coffee and cookies afterward. Still, Hallie's never been to one and she's young. *How will she take it?* I wonder.

"Who died?" Mrs. Prince asks.

"Sarah Davidson. She worked at the apple orchard ..."

"Oh my goodness." Mrs. Prince covers her mouth with her hand, her eyes large and suddenly shining. "She gave your sister's class the apple-picking tour last fall. But Sarah is so young."

"It was a car accident. Susan thinks it might be a faulty gas pedal. She has trouble with hers from time to time."

"Susan? Your school grandma?" Mrs. Prince asks.

I nod.

"She should tell the police. That's important information."

"Whatever," I say, again trying out my teen. Have I used the expression correctly? I admire Mrs. Prince and her strong beliefs and confidence, but I wonder what an older person, or a younger teen, for that matter, can ever say to the authorities that they might believe.

Mrs. Prince gets up and loads the dishwasher with the breakfast dishes.

The El-Q burbles its little musical note.

"You should teach that thing a better song." Mrs. Prince smiles.

"You're right," I answer, as I scan Hardeep's text wanting to know what I'm doing. Back and forth, thumbs flying, we arrange for him to come to the funeral, too. That boy will do anything to spend time with Hallie. He has less than twenty minutes to get ready.

I brush my teeth again, find the right boots in the hall closet, and before they are even on, Hardeep shows up at the door with frozen comb marks through his hair. He is wearing a navy pea coat over a shirt and tie and dress pants, and looks incredibly handsome — "hot" I suppose the younger generation would say.

"Is it okay to say you look really pretty today?" Hardeep asks.

I shrug my shoulders. "Why not?"

"Well, I dunno. You always look great. And it's a funeral …" he stumbles.

"Thank you," I answer. "You look nice, too."

We wait near the door together and I lean toward him, inhaling his spearmint breath. A loud honk causes us to jump apart as the Hurricane pulls up in the driveway.

"Bye, Mom!"

Hallie's mother rushes after me and I awkwardly kiss the cheek of a woman I barely know. Then I make a dash for the car, Hardeep at my side. The last thing I need is for Mrs. Prince to meet her real daughter in eighty-two-year-old form. The potential to recognize the personality of her child, even in an older body, is too great.

"Hi," I call out to Hallie and Linda and Margret as we squeeze into the back.

"You're wearing a dress?" Hallie, twisting around, asks me.

"Of course. It's a funeral," Margret grumbles from the front beside her. "Why wouldn't she dress up?"

"And you brought Hardeep?" Hallie squints at me.

"He wanted to come to support me," I answer.

"I hope that's all right," he says.

"Why not," she answers as though it's the most outlandish idea in the world.

I, on the other hand, am not surprised that my two friends are tagging along. I know Margret takes great comfort in funerals since her husband died. It's as though she needs an excuse to openly express her own grief. She likes to pretend to cry for others when she's still grieving for him. Linda will go out anywhere Margret or I go.

"It's at St. Gabriel's," says Hallie. But she doesn't put the car in gear. Instead, she stares for a long time at her house. Missing her family?

"Are you going to be okay?" I ask Hallie.

"Sure. I guess."

"A Catholic funeral. They'll have communion," I say, trying to prepare her. "It will be long."

Linda nods. "But the Ladies' Auxiliary there makes the best egg salad sandwiches."

"Better hurry up and go," Margret barks. "Parking will be tricky."

Hallie finally pulls away.

The drive proves quick and easy. The main streets are dry and clear with snowbanks neatly piled against the sidewalk. The parking lot and the church look full though — even the spots on the street are taken. The long black hearse sits in the front, waiting. We have to park on a side street and walk a block before entering the church.

Hallie looks out of place and confused so I hook my arm in hers and lead her to a back pew, Margret, Linda, and Hardeep following us. As we file in, I try to stay beside her but Margret and Linda shuffle around me so the seniors can all sit together. Hardeep ends up standing between Hallie and me.

While we are still arranging ourselves, a voice calls out a number and a title, "Be Not Afraid," and the organ starts. Margret quickly opens the hymnal and begins singing, her voice strong and melodic. The words of the song are uplifting: apparently even in a desert, we will never die of thirst. But they are sung so slow that it's still sad.

A young man in a white robe leads a procession with a golden crucifix held high in his hands. An older man, also in white, the priest, I suppose, walks slowly in front of a coffin. Draped in white like a banquet table, it is clearly on wheels, but eight people crowd around it, guiding it by the handles on all sides.

At the back, a young dark-haired girl pushes, tears streaked down her cheeks. Her sister? Kiera is her name, I recall from the obituary.

At the front, a tall glassy-eyed young man with clenched jaws pulls. Strongly resembling her, he must be her brother, Caleb. An older woman and a man follow, their hands clutching together tightly as they weep.

The pain is so raw.

The priest reads and then there is a prayer.

Hallie glances at Margret, who, even though she is not Catholic, kneels and crosses herself. But Margret has better knees than Linda and I ever did, so I stop Hallie as she begins her descent. Reach over Hardeep and grab her hand and hold it, squeezing. Willing her to feel my strength.

The service plods forward somberly with readings and prayers and hymns and then communion. Lineups of mourners shuffle to the steps of the altar, where they hold out their hands like beggars. Each is awarded a wafer, which they quickly swallow as they bow their heads.

Finally, the priest speaks about all the work Sarah did for the church community, including the Christmas drive delivering presents to children. The last drive Sarah made. The drive that is so crucial to us.

He calls up the young woman from the procession to say a few words. She begins, "My sister, Sarah, was the best sister a girl could have. If I needed to talk, or wanted help picking out clothes, she was always there for me. After she bought her new car last September, she drove me and my friends everywhere ..." She falters and begins to cry.

Perhaps it is remembering that driving killed her sister that causes the young woman to break down. Instantly, the young man rushes to her side and hugs her. The two of them stand cocooned together in their grief, unable to move away.

The older woman walks up and takes the paper from her daughter's hand. Eyes streaming, she reads a poem the girl wrote about her sister. Something about leaving an empty bedroom in the house and an empty place in their hearts. It is an utterly sad moment and both Margret and Linda cry. But Hallie's sobs bubble up uncontrollably.

I can't reach her but Hardeep does, immediately throwing his arms around this eighty-two-year-old senior. She cries on his shoulder.

Does Hallie now understand just how wonderful this young man is?

The priest leads a last liturgy as he shakes what looks like a golden lamp over the coffin. Here, there, over the feet, over the head. Only the lamp sheds no light; instead, it releases a choking sweet incense. When the pallbearers finally approach the coffin again, Sarah's father breaks down, his head and hands on the coffin, unable to let go.

Mrs. Davidson, weeping, gently tugs him up and they follow as it leaves. Rows upon rows of people file out. Besides learning that Sarah definitely drove a new car, none of this ceremony has given us the answers we need to mount a case against Saji Motors. All of it, the needless loss and sorrow, makes me want to scream at those car people. We have to pursue this to the end. I follow the crowd down into the basement reception area.

CHAPTER 25

Hallie

WHEN THE COFFIN LEAVES THE church, most people head downstairs directly for the reception. But I can't. Instead, I hobble outside, my Susan-legs stiff from the long sit, and take big breaths of air.

It was the part when Sarah's sister spoke that got to me. My sister, Aria, would have been sad like that if I had taken that ride on the roller coaster. I keep breathing deeply, hoping my chest will loosen up again.

Then I see her standing on the sidewalk: long, black, silky hair. She waves and I can almost make out the blue letters on her wrist. I know what they say. *Carpe Diem*. Eli in waitress form again.

"You are such a jerk!" I rush at her. "How can you let someone so young die? Why don't you bring her back? Let her have a full life. Look what you've done to her family!"

"Me?" Eli's eyebrows raise and she shakes her head. "I'm not the one who drove through a red light. I like to take the bus when I can. Keeps me in touch with people. Less of a carbon footprint."

"You know what I mean. Is this all some kind of joke to you?"

"Free will," Eli says, tapping her nose. "Doesn't work all that well for some people. So what are you going to do about this?"

"I'm just a kid. Well, an old lady right now. No one listens to either of us. What can I do?"

"I'm not going to give you step-by-step instructions."

"Really?" I'm sputtering I'm so mad. "You should have stayed a dog for all you're worth."

But Eli just tilts her head, calmly considering me. "Don't you like dogs? I could have done a cat."

I roll my eyes.

"Listen," she smiles and pats my shoulder, "you can keep trying. That's what it's all about. You never know when you can make a difference."

"But why can't you just tell me what to do? This is my free will asking you here."

"Listen to your inner voice." She winks and taps her nose again, turns and walks away.

Even though I want to grab her and shake her till she tells me more, I let her go. This person can make lightning come down and strike me, after all. She's annoyingly patient. Still angry, I head back into the church.

While I want to pound down the stairs and call out my questions before I lose my nerve, my knees and ankles creak as I slowly take each step to the reception area. I grip the railing for support and I think about my purpose here. Sarah Davidson bought a new Hurricane in the fall, we know that for certain. If she is Applegirl, we have to find proof. Eli isn't really to blame — she's right. Imagine, all this pain is caused by some flaw in their cars that Saji Motors refuses to admit. They can't be allowed to keep killing people with their faulty gas pedals.

Finally, I make it to the basement.

What to do? I look around. Margret and Linda sit at a table with some other older people, eating and chatting. Susan and Hardeep stand in line near Sarah's brother. Teens talking to another teen — that just makes sense. Except, will Susan's soul just spill old-lady-isms, using my tongue and mouth? Who knows. Maybe it won't make a difference. It shouldn't, anyway.

Eli said it's the effort that counts and she's trying.

Sarah's brother is good-looking. I wish I could be in my own body and talk to him.

But instead I make my way to Mr. and Mrs. Davidson, who have people lined up in front of them, too. One by one, they shake hands with them or hug them.

"So sorry for your loss."

"She's in a better place."

"Such a terrible thing. Parents should never outlive their children."

"God needed an angel."

The things people say.

I doubt if Eli really needs Sarah in angel form at this particular moment in time. Finally, I am up, directly in front of Sarah's mother. I take a breath. "Um, your daughter Sarah gave my sister the apple-picking tour at the orchard. She's in grade two."

Mrs. Davidson's eyes narrow, her brow furrows. I

instantly understand my mistake. How can someone so old have a seven-year-old sister?

I quickly correct myself. "Did I say *sister*? Silly me. Sarah gave my granddaughter the tour. Sarah was wonderful." I pause, I just said *was* and I can see Mrs. Davidson's eyes filling.

"Well, she's still wonderful," I correct myself again. I imagine Sarah on a ride somewhere at that carnival where Susan and I met. "Just not here on earth with us."

Now Mrs. Davidson totally breaks down and cries onto my shoulder. I don't know what to do. I pat her back.

"You really think there's another place after ...?" Mrs. Davidson asks when she lifts her head again.

"Oh, I know so," I tell her. Maybe, for once, looking old carries an advantage; it makes me seem wise.

She tries to smile while she blows her nose into a tissue.

I can't ask the poor lady questions about her dead daughter's car. Instead, I back away to let another friend of hers try to comfort her.

Nearby, Susan seems to be having a good conversation with Sarah's brother. I join her.

"Caleb, this is my adoptive grandmother, Susan. She drives a Hurricane just like your sister ..." *did.* She doesn't finish the sentence but I'm sure, just like me, Caleb does it in his head.

"Grandma, Caleb here tells me that his sister did have problems with her car. I'm sure she's the Applegirl you chatted with on the Saji Happy Motoring site."

"Did you tell the police about it?" I ask him.

"No. I never talked to the police. Should I?"

Next to us there's a lull in the conversation that suddenly makes Hardeep's next line sound out as clear and loud as a gong.

"Why would your sister run a red light?" He doesn't mean it as a challenge, but with the new-found volume, it maybe sounds like that, at least to Sarah's dad.

He turns and grabs Hardeep by the lapels, shaking him. "My daughter was a great driver. I don't care what anyone says."

CHAPTER 26

Susan

GENTLY, I LAY MY HANDS ON the grieving man's arms. "Come now," I say softly, trying to reason with him and soothe at the same time. My young voice fails on him; he raises Hardeep up on his toes.

"Hardeep didn't mean that the way you think," Hallie says from behind me. Coming from those eighty-two-year-old lips, the words sound calming and wise; even I want to listen.

His fists uncurl. Once the contact is broken, I quickly step in between them. That gives Mr. Davidson a moment to breathe hard and calm down. I feel safe, knowing he's not about to throttle me, a girl who's younger than the daughter he will be burying.

Mr. Davidson takes a step back.

"He, *we*, are all angry with the car manufacturer," Hallie says carefully. "We're sure Saji Motors is at fault."

"How is that possible?" Sarah's father sounds tormented. He pulls at his own hair from either side, completely breaking down. People close in around him, talking low, patting him. Sarah's mother breaks into the circle, reaches her arms around him, and they cry together.

Only just imagining their pain, my eyes fill up; swallowing becomes difficult. I have to back away. Losing my own sister was a huge blow but, thank Eli, my children are still alive, even though sometimes distant. I shake my head. I whisper to Hardeep and Hallie, "This isn't the right time. We're making it worse for them. We'd better go."

Hallie looks like she wants to disagree, but thankfully, she follows me as I move toward the stairs. I call out to Linda and Margret, who seem even more reluctant to leave. Still, they are dependent on the ride, and so they slowly stand up and push in their chairs. More slowly still, they follow us back up to the front-door exit.

"We can't give up on Applegirl's accident. It's too important!" Hallie says as we head to the Hurricane.

"You think Sarah's death is because of a gas pedal problem?" Linda asks from behind us. "You should let Saji Motors know, then!"

"Don't be so naive," Margret crabs at her, then clasps her hand on Hallie's shoulder, slowing her down. "We can go to the police with this information, right now."

"Exactly." I'm glad Margret agrees. She's always had a good head on her shoulders. "They're investigating the accident, after all. They should be able to take it from there."

We all finally straggle to the car and climb in.

"You don't need that thing," Margret complains when Hallie reaches for her El-Q. "I can direct you."

Hallie slips the device back into her purse.

Margret is right. It is a short, easy drive down the city streets after rush hour. I watch for any hesitations or surges when Hallie accelerates or brakes. But the Hurricane seems to perform well.

Suddenly, Hallie brakes and honks the horn loud.

I look around to find out why and see Chael and Kendra, startling apart from the noise.

I wave frantically, wanting Chael to know that I see him.

If he does, he ignores me.

But Hallie must now acknowledge that her crush is a player, at best, if not an outright cheat. Didn't that kiss at the pool mean something to him? I search Hallie's profile from the back seat to see any reaction. Nothing much. Of course, in a way, Hallie cheated, too. At least her body did. I have been holding hands and kissing Hardeep since Chael's kiss, but Hallie doesn't know that.

The Hurricane rolls forward again.

Hardeep gives me a small sympathetic smile. He takes my hand and squeezes it. I could love this boy if I were his age. Find it hard not to love him at the point in time I'm in now. But can Hallie?

Another block and we are at the police station. We drive past a parking lot half full of squad cars — black-and-white penguins lying in the snow — and pull into the visitors' parking.

I wish we could leave Margret and Linda behind, perhaps with the window open a crack. But it's winter and Margret likes to have her say in everything; Linda loves an adventure.

Instead, all of us head to the entrance of the large, beige concrete building where the doors automatically slide open and close silently behind us. We step into a spacious foyer with a black tile floor and walls the colour of winter sky. Rows of black fabric chairs sit near two counters. The sign above the long wood-grained one says it's for police checks. There seem to be many people behind it, working at computers. Ah, technology! So many screens to keep people from helping anyone.

The sign over the other, more of a cubical manned by a single officer, says it's for collision and other reporting. We stroll up to the lone police officer and wait for her to look up from her paperwork.

Margret coughs.

Finally, the officer puts her pen down. "How can we be of service today?" she asks.

Margret speaks up. "We have some important information regarding the car accident that occurred on Guelph Line a few days ago." Just as well she takes over.

Hallie is still an inexperienced teen in a geriatric body. I may have a mature soul but I look like a teen with potential attitude.

"Have a seat on the bench. Fill out this form, please." She hands Margret a clipboard and a stick pen. "I'll have an officer out to talk to you in a moment."

Margret turns the clipboard over to Hallie and a moment turns into fifteen minutes. Even with all her hesitation at filling in my personal information, Hallie returns the clipboard well before Officer Meryl Wilson steps in through the door.

"Oh my God!" Or perhaps I should say, *Oh my Eli*. My heart sinks. She's the one who gave Hallie the speeding ticket and wants my licence suspended.

Officer Wilson heads to the counter and talks to the person on duty there. When they finish their discussion, she heads our way.

She smiles, friendly enough, extending a large hand and reintroducing herself.

Only Hallie shakes it.

"I understand you have some information regarding the car accident we're investigating?" she says.

"Yes," Hallie answers.

"Follow me to the office, then."

We all squeeze into a tiny room with a desk and two chairs on opposite sides. Hallie quickly claims one — she needs it with her bad knees; the rest of us shuffle beside Hallie as Officer Wilson claims the other. With no personal photographs or memorabilia anywhere, the room feels like an interview closet rather than anyone's office. It smells vaguely of pine cleanser.

"So what information do you have regarding this case?" Officer Wilson asks, pulling up a screen on the computer.

"Sarah Davidson complained on the Saji Happy Motoring message board about her gas pedal," Hallie says.

"Oh, now I know why you look familiar. You're the lady who was speeding on the QEW the other day." She faces the screen and types something.

"Yes and I also explained about my accelerator sticking. We had the car towed to Saji Motors and they repaired it."

"Are you satisfied with the job?"

"The gas pedal seems to be working so far … but …"

Officer Wilson stops typing and folds her hands on the desk for a moment.

"On the message board, another person complained that the Saji repair didn't work for their vehicle. That the car still sped up on them," Hallie adds.

"Do you have their contact information?" Officer Wilson asks.

"Not exactly. The person went by the name Applegirl."

"We think Applegirl is Sarah Davidson's handle," Hardeep adds.

"Her nickname on the message board," I explain in case she's as uninformed about these things as I am.

The officer stares at Hallie as though waiting for more information. Then she nods. "All right. We can have our IT department look at the site. They can establish her identity more definitely."

"Yes, but …" Hallie says.

Hardeep finishes for her. "Those posts have all disappeared."

Officer Wilson frowns.

"We think Saji Motors took them down. They are deliberately withholding this information from the public," I tell her.

Officer Wilson shakes her head. "So we don't have any evidence at all."

"We all saw the site. We can be witnesses," Hardeep insists.

"That is something," Officer Wilson says. "But it may not be enough. We need to get a subpoena to ask Saji for their website information. The judge may not feel this is enough to go on."

"What else do we need?" Hallie asks. "Her brother knows she was having accelerator problems. She ran a red light."

"None of that proves the gas pedal stuck at the time. What we really need is an eyewitness, preferably in the car at the time."

"Aw man, Sarah is dead," Hallie says, sounding more teen than she should for a senior. "If she had another passenger, he or she would be dead, too."

"I have to agree," I say. "It sounds like Saji Motors will get away with this forever. And their cars are killing people."

CHAPTER 27

Hallie

"YOU COULD CALL YOUR SON AND see if there's something he can do," Susan tells me as we walk out of the building. Then she turns to Hardeep. "Her son is a lawyer."

"Yes, I remember," Hardeep says as we head toward the Hurricane. "Should make things a lot easier."

"Not necessarily," Susan answers him. "Lawyers can be a lot harder to convince … uh, so I've heard, anyway."

"He is stubborn," I agree, playing along. What do I really know, anyway? I shrug my shoulders as we reach the car. "Let me just text him. I don't want to disturb him if he's in court or something," My standard cover. A phone set on vibrate shouldn't disturb him at all. I just want to avoid talking directly to people who know Susan really well. Ron already thinks she's ready for the home, and every time I screw up, I only make things worse.

Went to Sarah Davidson's funeral. Found out she had gas pedal issues. Police say this is not enough. What do you think?

The El-Q burps instantly. So much for avoiding actual talking.

"Mom, you went to some strange person's funeral?" Ron repeats.

Again, whatever I do makes Susan seem senile to him. "Hello, honey. How are you?" I answer sarcastically. It's what my mom does all the time to me if I hit her up for money or a lift without a chat first.

"I'm fine, you?" he says apologetically.

"Good, thank you for asking." I roll my eyes for Hardeep and Susan's sake. They open the car doors, and one by one, everyone climbs back in. I get into the driver's seat and turn the key so that the car will get warm.

"So this funeral," he starts in again.

I cut him off. "The Davidsons give all the apple picking tours to schools in the area. Everyone knows them. Linda and Margret wanted to go, too. Heck, they go to lots of funerals of people they don't know." I'm making the last part up. But from the looks of how much they enjoyed the food and conversation, it sounds like something they would do.

"But you asked these people who were grieving about their child's death whether her gas pedal stuck?"

"Not me personally. My adoptive granddaughter Hallie did."

"You brought your new teenager friend along?" From the tone in Ron's voice, I can hear he thinks this is demented, too, as in coming from an old person possibly getting dementia.

"She's my technology buddy. Remember, she's getting her volunteer hours in. Ron, my two young friends actually saw that post on the Saji Happy site. They can testify about the gas pedal complaints."

Ron sighs loudly on the phone.

Susan nudges me from the back seat and whispers, "Ask him about a class-action suit."

"Ron, tell me what it would take for you to sue Saji Motors."

"Well, as you know, I practise a different kind of law."

Whoops!

He pauses. "And the allegations you're making against a major car company are serious. You need strong evidence. No one would take this on without that."

"What's strong evidence? Applegirl died."

"More accidents, for one. I mean you can't have a class action without a few victims, more than two certainly. Eye-witnesses who actually feel that gas pedal sticking during the accident would help, too."

"But these car crashes are fatal. Unless people come back from the dead, we don't have any witnesses." When you think about it, Susan and I have done just that. Of course, if I told him about visiting that carnival in the other world, he'd order up an ambulance to deliver me straight to Sunnyside.

"On another note, Mom ..." Ron sounds uneasy and hesitates. "Can we talk about something else for a minute?"

"You can't change the subject, Ron. This is important."

"All right, all right. I'll ask a colleague who works on these things. But what I have to discuss is important, too."

I suddenly know what he's going to talk about and

I feel a little sick. There's nothing I can do to save Susan from this. In fact, everything I say or do pushes Ron further toward this idea.

"Would you look at another residence with me? This one's near Tansley Woods. Elmwood Village. You could still go to Aquafit with your friends, visit the library. You'd never even have to get into a car."

My mouth buckles as I look up into my own green eyes reflected from the rear-view mirror. Susan's eyes currently. They look so bright and happy, hopeful. "Sure," I answer, discouraged, wishing there were some other answer he would accept.

"Well, that's great. Sheryl will be so pleased." Now his words rush out quickly. "I promise you'll like this one. The units have lots of light; they're individual apartments with little kitchens. You cook your own meals if you like or buy a dining plan ..."

I've made this all too easy for him, I can tell, so I backtrack. "That is, I'll look at this residence if you promise to keep an open mind on the Saji Motors lawsuit. And ... my friend Hallie can come."

"But Hallie is a teenager! Why don't you bring Linda and Margret, instead? You could all put your names on the list. Think how much fun it would be if your friends lived there too."

"Hallie's coming. I want her opinion." But of course, what I need is Susan's thoughts on this residence. Hopefully, she will be the one who lives her life out there if our souls return to our bodies.

"Fine. Five o'clock at the condo sound okay?"

"Let me check with Hallie and get back to you. Love you." I hang up before he can argue.

"He wants you to look at homes?" Margret repeats as I put the El-Q into my bag.

"Yes."

"But if you move out of your condo, we won't be able to do the crossword together," Linda says.

"Or get a lift to the pool," Margret says.

"She's going to lose her driver's licence, anyway," Susan says, sounding annoyed as she tells them, "if she can't convince the judge about the gas pedal sticking."

"Ron thinks you both might want to sign onto the waiting list, too," I tell the old ladies.

Linda's eyes pop and her jaw drops.

"I'm too young," Margret snaps.

Linda struggles. "Um, um, but it's so far from the mall."

"They provide buses for that." Neither of them looks convinced. *Too bad*, I think. *Susan will have to go in there alone. Unless* . . . "You know, they usually provide a nice free meal for guests who want to tour."

"I could check my calendar," Margret offers.

"I know I'm free," Linda says.

"I will come with if Hallie wants me to," Hardeep says.

Visiting an old-age home just so he can be with me, or at least Susan in my body — it breaks my heart. Susan texts my mother to let her know where we're going and that she won't be home for supper.

She reads the answer text out loud. *Be home by ten. Love you.*

When I hear those last two simple words, I miss my family so badly that I have trouble swallowing. I blink hard.

"Maybe you should call your son," Susan says gently. "Tell him we can make it and give him numbers."

All together there are five of us, now. I have doubts this will make Ron happy, so again, I text him instead of calling. Less chance of an argument that way.

Hallie will come with us to tour the residence. Her friend Hardeep, and Margret and Linda, too. All expecting free dinner. Please arrange. Love Mom XXOO.

Then I put the Hurricane into drive and we head back to the condo to wait for Ron.

CHAPTER 28

Susan

I WATCH AS HALLIE DRIVES EVER so carefully down Upper Middle, slowing well in advance of lights or stop signs, gently, gently speeding up again. "How will we ever get an eye-witness to a gas pedal failure," I wonder out loud from the back of the car.

"What we need is a video," Hardeep suggests. "A dash cam could show when a driver loses control of the gas."

"Hey, that's a great idea!" Hallie points a wrinkled finger at Hardeep in the mirror. "We can use the El-Qs if we have another problem."

"Maybe we should try forcing the issue," I say. "We could try stopping and starting hard when there's no one around."

"That sounds very unsafe," Margret grumbles. "Here, let me have that thing." She reaches for my purse in the front seat and removes the device. "How do I start this again?"

Hardeep reaches over the seat and sets it up. "Now you just need to press the red circle when you want the video to begin."

Margret reaches down, presumably to video the gas pedal. "Can't really see if your foot is pushing down or not."

"The driver will just have to narrate the video," Hallie says. "Hey, the mall lot looks empty right now. I'm going to turn in and try braking hard."

Margret shakes her head. "You can't be serious."

"Oh, this is exciting!" Linda clasps her hands together as we enter into the lot. "Like solving a mystery."

"Won't Ron mind if we're late?" I ask. Of course, I know how much he hates other people's tardiness. It's a waste of his time and he has so little of it.

"We won't be. We'll just try once. Ready, Margret? Turn on the video."

Margret aims the El-Q camera on Hallie, who, behind the steering wheel, talks to an unknown audience.

"I'm Susan MacMillan and I'm going to test out the gas pedal on my Hurricane this afternoon. It's been into Saji Motors twice. Computer diagnosis said nothing was wrong. The second time, mechanics cleaned the electronic throttle plate and installed a reinforcement bar. On the Saji message board, other drivers complained that the repairs did not help with the problem.

"I will hit the brake pedal hard, then switch back to the gas, then hit the brake again. One driver thought this pattern would cause the sticking."

Without further warning, the Hurricane stops abruptly. Hardeep's head snaps forward in perfect synchronicity with mine. Before either of our heads flop back again, the Hurricane shoots away.

"Is it stuck?" Panic edges Margret's words. "Can you make it slow down?" She ducks her head and covers it with her hands, the El-Q still in one of them. "You're going to drive into the store!"

"I'm switching from the gas pedal to the brake again. It's all working like it's supposed to." Hallie sounds disappointed. "The Hurricane is slowing down."

"If the gas pedal stuck consistently" — I give everyone my standard line, the one no one seems to listen to — "it would be easy to prove there's a defect."

"And report it," Linda adds.

"Well, I'm not holding this thing forever." Margret turns off the El-Q and shoves it back in the purse on the seat.

"You know, we could get a dash mount in the IQ store," Hardeep suggests.

"You're going to be so late for Ron. He'll put you in a home for sure," I warn Hallie.

"Why don't I run in?" Hardeep suggests. "You go ahead and meet your son and bring him back here. Won't take more than ten minutes."

"I'll go too," I offer.

From the rear-view mirror, Hallie gives me the eye. The watery grey-blue aged eye that knows and sees all. She's a smart girl; she must understand I want her to go out with Hardeep rather than Chael. That if I win her a boy, Hardeep will be the one. But it shouldn't matter. Right now, we have to figure out how to get back into our own bodies again if any kind of romance is to happen.

"Okay." Hallie reaches into my purse and pulls out a credit card. "You can pay with this. We'll meet you back at this door."

I snatch up the card and jump out the back, enjoying the energy and spring in my knees and ankles. The winter air bites, and my nose hairs clamp. Hardeep grabs my hand, and we run through the snow, over the sidewalk, and in through the mall doors. A blast of heat hits us, then that curious odour, like burnt wire or perhaps the smell of money burned up in technology. The smell of the IQ store.

We enter together and the same wide-jawed girl greets us. Mandi is her name; how can I ever forget it? But does Mandi remember us? I hope not. And if she does, will she hover nearby, hoping to catch us shoplifting?

"Is there anything I can help you with?" Mandi asks.

"We need a dash mount for an El-Q," Hardeep answers.

Mandi points to the back of the store. "Ask Matt. He's over at the Intelligence Bar."

Hardeep leads the way. He greets Matt at the bar; the very same Matt who nearly had me arrested last visit.

"We were told you have the El-Q car mount," I tell him.

Behind his thick glasses, Matt's oversized grey eyes focus. I'm almost sure he must recognize me as the girl the security guards tried to cart away. But he says nothing, just reaches to the back wall and puts the mount on the counter.

I tap the credit card to pay.

Matt raises an eyebrow. How many fifteen-year-olds have a Visa, after all? "Do you want a bag?" is all he says.

"No, thank you." I rush out of the store with Hardeep alongside of me. I'm not even out of breath at the end of our jog back to the mall exit.

He pushes the door open, and I'm relieved to see we've beaten the Hurricane back to our meeting place. As we wait for the car to return, we huddle close for warmth. I can smell that hint of spearmint on Hardeep's breath cloud.

"Where are they?" After a few minutes, I have to stomp my feet to keep my toes warm.

He smiles. His eyes hold mine.

The realization comes over me that we have some alone time again, and I can't help but smile back. This handsome young boy. I should really resist.

But he leans forward and wraps my shoulders with his arms. Before I can pull out of his grasp, he tilts his head and draws his face to mine.

From the corner of my eye, I spot the Hurricane, but I don't care. I close the gap and touch my lips to his.

My lips part, his slacken too. I can taste his sweetness now. Can I keep this moment forever?

The horn blasts. Of course, Ron is driving. No patience for anybody or anything.

We break apart but I lift my hand to my mouth, trying to hold the feeling there a while longer.

Hardeep circles to the passenger side where Hallie sits. He leans across her to lift and lower a lever against the dash so that the new mount will stick.

Hallie tests it, and when she sees it holds, slides her El-Q into the mount and adjusts it to face Ron.

"Mom, we're late as it is," Ron complains. "I'm not going to sing so you can post it on YouTube."

"This is just in case the accelerator malfunctions. You can document the event," Hallie explains. "People would believe you. You're a middle-aged man and a lawyer, too."

He shakes his head as we pull away. Ron drives hard, rolling through stop signs, rushing through yellow lights, but we never really hit any reds. He gets on the highway, even though Tansley Woods is only a few long city blocks away. The speedometer needle hits 110, slow enough not to be stopped for speeding. "Accelerator works fine for me," he comments as he turns on the first exit ramp. We're in the Elmwood Village parking lot by 5:30.

Ron smiles as he checks his cellphone. "Good. Only fashionably late." He turns to Hallie. "Now Mom. This is really the perfect spot. You are going to love it. Just promise me that you will keep an open mind."

CHAPTER 29

Hallie

IT'S HARD TO KEEP AN OPEN MIND when someone tries so hard to sell you on an idea. Kind of makes you want to run in the other direction. But Ron never lets up. As we step into the entrance of the complex, he throws his arms open wide. "Will you just look at these windows? Can you imagine how bright this place is in the daytime?"

Susan nods as she looks around. Don't tell me he's selling her?

Still, the building looks new and the neutral beige walls and dark wood decor give the entrance a calm feel. None of that pink-and-blue lilacy-ness that Sunnyside had.

A tall, tan-skinned lady with a long black ponytail rushes out of an office to greet us. Ron introduces us. "Mom, this is Briana Amil; Briana, this is my mother, Susan MacMillan."

Smiling brilliantly, she offers me a slender hand. We shake and she has a nice grip, not knuckle crushing and yet not floppy and fishlike.

Margret, Linda, Hardeep, and Susan shake hands with her, too, and give her their names. Well, of course, Susan gives her mine.

Briana then guides us through the Elmwood "town centre," a wide hall lined on both sides with various shops and services.

Linda oohs and ahhs over the huge fieldstone fireplace in the library.

Ron tells me I can donate all my books, and in this way, new friends I make can share in my favourite stories.

New friends. Those words make Linda flinch.

Susan frowns and grows quiet.

When we pass the hairdressing salon, Margret stops to peek in. "How much does it cost for a perm?"

The lady hands her a list of prices.

Margret scans it and snorts. "I have a young woman who comes to my home and does it for less." She folds the paper and tucks it into her purse.

Briana leads us into the lounge, where a huge screen covers one wall. "*The Second Best Exotic Marigold Hotel* is playing tonight. It's a favourite with residents." She shrugs. "Richard Gere."

"Can anyone come to the movie night? I mean guests, family, friends?" Susan asks.

As if, I think. No one will want to visit a home full of old people.

"I'd like to see Richard Gere," Linda says.

"Full house tonight, I'm afraid — movie nights are quite popular. Non-residents can attend, you just need reservations," Briana answers.

Next, she shows us a craft kitchen where inmates can, say, bake cookies on activity days. "But of course, in the apartments, you will have your own fridge and stove."

"Apartments?" Margret repeats, looking intrigued.

"Yes. We have several levels of care at Elmwood. You can have independent living with housekeeping and linens done for you."

"I hate laundry!" Margret chimes in.

"Then, if you want more assistance, you can add a meal package. Or add one because you hate cooking." She takes us to an elevator next. "One of the residents offered to let you see his apartment." She keys in a code and the door slides open. We step in and she asks me to press three. It's a quiet, slow ride up. "Good evening," she calls to a couple who come on just as we are leaving.

They're sweet, the woman's arm tucked into the man's. Both wear silver-wired glasses and similarly styled jackets in pale blue and yellow. It's as though living together makes their tastes blend and turn into one style.

"Mr. and Mrs. Flavelle got married in the chapel right here at Elmwood last year," Briana tells us as we turn down the hall.

"Really?" Margret asks.

"It looks like they've been together forever," Linda comments.

"I hate when couples dress alike," Susan grumbles.

"How are you, Aiden?" Briana calls to a tall thin man with tubes in his nose.

"All right, thanks." He smiles and continues to the elevator.

"You keep young people in here?" Margret squawks once he's gone.

"Anyone who needs assistance," Briana answers. "We're called 'long term' but we also offer respite care when families need help with their loved ones. Perhaps when they go on holidays ..."

We arrive at a door marked 307 and Briana knocks. "Gord? Are you there?"

Gord? Could it be?

It is! Spinach-salad dude opens up. "Hello there, come on in." He sweeps us in with his hand. Gord looks different, more formal. No Santa hat, plus he's wearing a sports jacket and a bow tie. Kind of handsome for an old dude. Did he dress for us especially?

"Hey, Susan! Margret, Linda. What a nice surprise! I didn't realize it was you girls who were checking out my pad."

Girls. He is talking about women over eighty, the only girls he knows. Except for me, of course — at least my soul is girl-age.

"We didn't know you lived here," Linda answers as we look around.

Susan smiles again. Guess Gordon living here is a big plus.

Instantly, I like this apartment better than that room at Sunnyside. It's bigger, for one.

"That's the bathroom," Gord says and opens the door.

"The tub and shower are easy entry with safety handles to make it senior friendly," Briana offers.

"Can I take as many baths and showers as I like?" I ask, remembering the only-two-in-one-week rule at Sunnyside.

"Of course," Briana answers. "That's what independent living means."

Gord grins. "It's the best. I go as I please. Walk to Aquafit and the library. Join a card game if I want, or any of the Village events." He tugs at both sides of his bow tie and waggles his eyebrows. "Tonight I'm taking my daughter to dinner and a show."

"Why, that's wonderful!" Susan says, and I nudge her. Her words sound suspiciously old coming from my young body.

"But for those with less mobility," Briana continues, "retirement living units offer a complete meal plan and light help with dressing, bathing, and medications."

Medications! Drat, I forgot Susan's pills.

"We also have an assisted-living floor plus a long-term-care ward for those with memory issues."

I'm fifteen and I already forget things. Oh well, I'll just have to take all that medication later, before bed.

"All of our units come with emergency response systems."

Margret snorts again. "When my husband died, my son ordered me one of those senior alarm systems."

"That's what I want for Mom," Ron says. "Until she makes up her mind about residences."

"Well, it went off in the middle of the night for no reason," Margret continues, "and this voice told me it was sending an ambulance. I told them I didn't need one, to cancel the alert. Then I went back to sleep. Next thing I knew, another voice was talking at me. Telling me they were sending someone to wait with me till the ambulance arrived."

"That's terrible!" Briana chuckles. "Our system's not like that. One of our staff comes to your aid instantly. No voices over intercoms."

"But how else can seniors live alone?" Ron asks. "What if Mom has a heart attack at her condo in the middle of the night?"

"She has us," Margret insists. "We check on her every morning, bright and early."

"They do look in on me early, early," I tell Ron.

Something chimes and Gord unflips a phone. "Hi, Honey, you almost here?" His smile drops. "Sure. I understand. If Brendon's not feeling well … you can't help that. Love you, too!" He snaps the phone shut.

We're all silent for a moment. It's so obvious he's been stood up.

Then Susan pipes up. "Hey, would you like to join us for a bite to eat?"

Margret and Linda turn to look at her. A fifteen-year-old asking a senior dude to dinner does seem a little odd. Especially with the way she is looking at him.

"That's okay. You guys are all together. You don't need me tagging along."

"But you're dressed so smart." She rubs my young hand over his sleeve.

Okay, that is really weird. I know what I have to do to make this right. "Yes, please dine with us, Gordon." I try to talk older-lady style. "You can advise on what to order. Give us your insight on what it's like to live here."

"Well, if you put it that way! Sure. That would be great." His smile lifts up again.

We check out the small living room and the bedroom, which overlooks the parking lot. The galley kitchen, too — everything is neat and clean. Why not? He has a cleaning service. Still, he made that great spinach salad.

"Any questions?" Briana asks.

I shake my head.

"How much does it cost?" Margret asks. "I heard living here is as expensive as living on a cruise ship."

"Oh no, no, no," Gord answers. "You heard that wrong. People say it's as much *fun* as living on a cruise ship."

Briana smiles. "Price point depends on the size of apartment and level of care you choose. I can get you some brochures if you're considering Elmwood for yourself."

Margret nods.

"If we're all done here, then let's head for the dining room. They're expecting us."

We follow Gord out of the apartment and back to the elevator. Brenda's, the name of the restaurant, is up on the tenth floor.

The elevator chimes and the doors slide back as we arrive. A short walk to the left gets us to the door, where the hostess greets us.

"What a fabulous view!" Ron comments as we enter.

Much as I want to disagree, it *is* nice, like we're on top of the world. Large windows overlooking snow-topped roofs and Christmas lights. In the centre is a gas fireplace lighting up and warming the room.

A large table is reserved for us and the hostess seats us immediately. A server asks if we want something to drink and Briana orders a bottle of wine.

Linda asks if she can also have a tea.

Instantly, the server comes back with glasses of water for everyone and a little white teapot for Linda, which amazes Margret to no end. "Usually, restaurants serve hot water in little metal pots with spouts. They leave the tea bags separate."

In a moment the server returns with the wine and pours for all the adults.

Margret sips at hers. "Mmm. Haven't had a glass of wine since my Ken died." She smiles.

That smile tugs at my heart. For the first time, I feel just a little sorry for grumpy old Margret.

The server returns, lists off the specials, and then hands us a menu that rivals the one at that chi-chi Perspectives I made Susan take me to a few days ago.

"Doesn't the food come included?" Margret gasps. "Just look at the prices of these entrées!"

"Don't worry, it's my treat," Ron says.

I can't help but enjoy this bit of revenge on Ron.

Briana jumps in. "With your unit rental, you can get a monthly food credit. Many residents prefer to make their own breakfasts or go out to lunch with friends. So this credit can usually cover the balance of their meal needs."

I want to order the fish and chips like Hardeep and Susan, but know already that I have a senior's digestive system. Instead, I copy Linda and have the Pacific halibut; Ron chooses the meatloaf and Margret gets the Lobster Benedict.

When we're all served, Briana raises her glass and waits for all of us to do the same. "To new beginnings."

"New beginnings," everyone mumbles back.

New endings for Susan and me are what I'm really wondering about and when Eli will make them happen. I sip at the wine.

Bleh! Stuff tastes like spoiled grape juice, although Linda and Margret guzzle. I've never seen Margret so happy.

Then Gord smiles at me. He's a sweet old guy but he doesn't stop. On the second sip of wine, I see where this is heading.

"Would you like to go to the movie with me this evening?"

CHAPTER 30

Susan

GORD ASKED ME OUT! AT LEAST he asked the eighty-two-year-old body that really belongs to me.

Or is it Hallie's fifteen-year-old soul that attracts him? Regardless of which, Hallie's the one who has to answer him. For the first time, I want to be back in my creaky old shell so I can be friends with people my own age again, and I can say yes!

How will Hallie handle this, though? I watch her.

"Ordinarily, I would love to go with you." Hallie sips at a glass of water. "Really, I would." Her pale skin seems to turn a different shade, grey perhaps? An invitation to a movie has this much of an effect on her? "But I'm not feeling myself." She turns to my son. "Ron, I think you should take me home."

What? But she should encourage Gord's companionship. A man who is funny and has great dance moves and makes wonderful salad, when will we ever meet someone like that again? We'll need companionship, whichever body we end up in.

"Sure, Mom, I'll take you home just as soon as I pay the bill." There's that tinge of annoyance to his tone. He doesn't believe Hallie, either. Probably he thinks it's a ruse to get away from the residence and further discussion of moving here.

"Are you okay?" Gord asks.

Hallie dabs at her face with the serviette. She sounds quite breathless when she answers him. "Fine, just really tired."

I don't believe she is play-acting anymore. Why is my old body sweating so much?

Briana waves the server over and Ron hands her a credit card. We grab our coats, and in moments, we are out the door, no dessert, no coffee.

"Can I get your phone number, so I can call later and make sure you're okay?" Gord asks as we head toward the elevator.

Hallie doesn't even answer him. Can't, it seems, as she continues to hyperventilate. She fans herself with her Elmwood brochure now. "I need to get some air," she pants.

"Don't worry," Margret addresses Gord, "she won't be alone. I'll sit with her tonight till she falls asleep."

Hallie still doesn't answer.

Ron squints at Hallie now, frowning. Looks like he's worried, too. He pulls a business card from his pocket and hands it to Gord. "Here. You can call me later. Thank you for your concern."

Gord gets off at the ground floor with us.

Hardeep says he can find his own way home from the residence. "Hope you feel better," he tells the real Hallie and gives me a quick peck on the cheek before taking off.

Gord continues with us all the way to the parking lot, where he shivers in his sports jacket as we climb into the car. Coming straight from his apartment, he's not wearing a winter jacket.

I think someone should insist he go back inside; he's going to catch his death of a cold. But instead he stands watching Hallie's grey face as the Hurricane pulls away, giving us all a sad wave.

Ron drives down Walker's Line to the QEW. Fast. I look around his shoulder toward the speedometer. Not even on the highway yet, and he's speeding.

"Hey, look over there!" Linda points to the field near the on-ramp of the expressway. "Isn't that the crazy hairless dog we took to the pound yesterday?"

I glance over, spot the wild black tufts of fur on the otherwise pink body, and realize she is right. *What does that mean?* I wonder. Why is Eli showing himself to us now? There's a reason. There has to be. A cold finger runs down my spine. "Better turn the El-Q on," I warn Hallie.

Struggling, Hallie pulls it from the purse. She slumps for a few moments, breathing hard. Finally, she reaches and mounts the El-Q on the dash, switches it on, and then collapses back against the seat, clutching at her arm.

Ron glances over at her. "Mom, you don't look so great. Maybe you should take some nitroglycerine."

"I'm fine," Hallie gasps.

But I know that she doesn't recognize what a heart attack feels like. Not caring what anyone makes of it, I unbuckle my belt now, reach over the seat, and grab the purse. Pulling out the vial of nitroglycerine, I tell her, "Open your mouth and lift your tongue."

Hallie does as she is told.

I shake out a pill and pop it in Hallie's mouth.

The nitroglycerine tumbles out. Hallie's too weak to keep it in.

Ron grabs for it and the Hurricane wobbles back and forth for a moment. I feel myself being tossed from side to side and he misses the catch. Hallie's head lolls to the side. "I'm taking you to the hospital!" Ron says. The Hurricane surges.

I get thrown backward but immediately scramble forward again.

That's when it happens. A small pink-and-grey creature darts onto the highway and stops directly in the Hurricane's path.

Eli.

His black eyes stare straight at the windshield, the tuft of hair on his head standing up defiantly.

"Don't stop!" I warn Ron, grabbing his shoulder. We don't have to do everything Eli wants. Free will after all. Ron doesn't even like animals; this should be easy for him.

But he doesn't listen.

Instead, he brakes hard, then steers wildly to the left.

Nobody's there, we're all safe.

But then he hits the gas pedal again, and the Hurricane leaps forward.

A few car lengths ahead, a gas tanker crawls along too slowly for the fast lane. There's nowhere for the Hurricane to move to at the pace we are travelling.

"Damn!" Ron's body slams back against the seat as his right leg straightens down.

To our right, an eighteen-wheeler rumbles along, effectively boxing us in.

"Move it!" Ron yells as he leans on the horn. Like a tuba hitting a sour note, it blasts out at the world. Neither truck makes a space for us. "I can't slow down. The gas pedal's sticking!"

The gap between us and the tanker closes rapidly.

I know from our last experience that the shoulder on the right side of the highway can accommodate us. But we can't get to it. That stupid eighteen-wheeler won't budge.

On the left side is a concrete guardrail.

We're going to hit the tanker.

Last minute, Ron steers hard toward the concrete barrier. The Hurricane slams into the cement.

There's a crash and a double gunshot.

Two small white clouds burst open in the front, then deflate like bubble gum. The airbags. Smoke fills the air. Without my seatbelt on, I bounce hard against the window, then the seat, then the window again.

The Hurricane rebounds off the cement and flips to its side, sliding back across four lanes of traffic. Miraculously, no one hits us and the car scrapes to a rest on the shoulder.

The darkness fades and I feel the sun warm on my face and the cool grass and hard ground beneath me. Where am I? Slowly I manoeuvre to my feet, hands holding my knees and pushing up. With a start, I notice my wrinkled, spotted hands. Oh no! I am back in my decrepit old shell. An organ plays, happy tinkling notes. In front of me stands a behemoth of a roller coaster. I see Eli in grubby carnival-worker mode, standing at the gate holding out his hand.

In front of him, Hallie, back in her young body, reaches to hand him a ticket.

"Noooo!" I scream and rush for them. She cannot get on that roller coaster! Before the piece of paper leaves Hallie's fingers, I snatch it away. "This is not a new ending. You will not die in a car accident on my watch!"

Eli looks at me patiently. "You hold the ticket now. Is this how you want the end to play?"

I hesitate. So many new things to experience out there. I can visit my granddaughter on my phone now. I could go to the movies with Gord.

Hallie jumps in. "I'm not going back there without her."

I sigh. I would miss Ron, maybe even Sheryl. But surely, it's my time. "Hallie, I'm eighty-two years old. If there's one ticket, I'm the one who should use it."

"But I'm the one who forgot to take your heart medication."

"The day we met for the first time, I was supposed to die of a heart attack. Remember?"

"But we have to fight Saji Motors together." Hallie sniffs and wipes at her eyes.

"Don't you dare cry for me. Do you hear me?" I grip Hallie's shoulders. "You gave me three extra days in a wonderful young body. Two boys kissed me. Two!"

"Always with the boys," Eli complains. "That wasn't supposed to be the goal, remember?"

Hallie snorts through the tears now.

I blink hard so I don't cry, too. I'm going to miss this adoptive granddaughter I've gotten to know inside out. "You don't need me to fight Saji. The whole thing must be recorded on your El-Q. And my son, Ron, will never let them get away with this." An awful thought hits me then. I look around. "Please tell me he is all right?" I don't see him anywhere near the roller coaster. "Are the others okay?"

Eli shrugs his shoulders. "This is not their voyage."

An elusive answer. Ron never liked rides, not even as a young boy. I look back toward the food stands. Ron would be wanting cotton candy. I see people standing in lines, some familiar, some not. Living this long, I've already lost so many friends and relatives. But he's not there amongst them. I feel a whoosh of relief. I scan the carousel and see some of my old friends but not Margret or Linda, and they like that kind of ride.

"Just Hallie and I died? And she's really only here because I removed her seatbelt."

"Details, details!" Eli throws up his hands. "Time to get on the roller coaster. Both of you! It's starting up in moments."

"No." I fling the ticket to the ground. "Neither of us is riding today."

"What?" Eli pulls his head back like a rooster ready to peck. "I thought you wanted to die. You never expected to grow this old, remember? You hate your aching joints, your wrinkly skin, your failing memory, your lack of energy, on and on ... complaints, complaints."

"Doesn't everyone complain?"

"Oh yes. 'Look at my fat thighs.' 'Why does my hair have to go frizzy?' 'I have a zit in the middle of my forehead.' So tiresome, so boring."

"Look who's complaining now!" I tell him.

Eli rolls his eyes.

"I'll never say another bad thing about my body," Hallie says. "It's perfect."

I fold my arms. "I'm not making any promises."

"Susan!" Hallie protests.

"I mean, I am grateful, Eli. People die of cancer when they're very young. I've raised my children. I could go now ..." I hesitate. "If one person must ride, it definitely should be me."

"So what contribution will either of you make that justifies keeping you on earth?" Eli asks.

"I definitely want to be on the witness stand against Saji Motors. That Applegirl should never have died," I answer.

"Me, too," Hallie says.

"We already established that Ron would take this case on and probably doesn't need either of you to testify."

"I want to have more time with my children and grandchildren," I admit.

"I can help seniors. Margret and Susan and any other older person who doesn't know how to use an iPad or e-reader. They can talk to their kids all over the world," Hallie answers.

Eli tilts his head, raises his eyebrows. "I do so love technology."

"Well, that's not all," Hallie continues. "I want to be a lawyer and fight companies that don't care about safety or the environment. The Saji thing would only be a start."

"Okay, somewhat better than your usual boy obsession." Eli turns.

"Sue me for being interested in Chael, really," Hallie says sarcastically. "It was never so much him or any boy as much as, I dunno ..." She flutters her hand in front of her face. "Feeling all jittery and breathless and having my heart race."

"Feeling in love," I fill in for her.

"Yes. Not the Mom and Dad kind but, you know, the love where someone, maybe just for a short while, chooses you over everybody else. Loans you his jacket and holds your hand."

"The love of my family would be enough for me," I say. "But I will say I enjoyed the pursuit of those young men. Their kisses. Hallie should have the chance to experience that someday."

"Okay, I can understand." Eli nods thoughtfully at Hallie, then turns to me. "What if you have to go into long-term care?"

"There's no question. I do have to move into a retirement residence. I don't want to be alone when I have a heart attack. I need help."

"What if you're different now? Much worse."

The question makes me stop and think for a moment. I look up at the bright blue sky without a single cloud in it. I look around and see people on the carousel or wild tea-cup ride. *Dead people?* I wonder. Waiting to move on to who knows what? "If I'm worse, then certainly, long-term care. Someone else can make my meals."

"You may need a wheelchair."

Worse and worse. I shut my eyes tightly. Maybe I should let it all go.

"Come back with me, please!"

My eyelids flip open again to see Hallie clasping her hands together, almost in prayer. She's so young, so tender-hearted. I sigh. I want to live on awhile longer for this granddaughter especially, so she doesn't have to experience my death right now. "Can it be one of those motorized scooters instead? I'll stick a red flag on it and drive it down the middle of the road."

Eli smiles. "I'll see what I can arrange."

CHAPTER 31

Hallie

"HALLIE, HALLIE!" MARGRET'S VOICE calls. Where is she calling from? Is it me she really wants? Am I in my own body? Something hard digs into my back, and as I reach around to feel what it is — a door handle — my eyes open and I see my own true skin again. Mmm. A deep sigh of relief. Then I lift myself up, bumping into somebody's legs. Linda's. She hangs in front of me unconscious, still strapped in her seat, mid-bench.

I blink, to make the setting in front of me clearer. I turn my head. The world seems so upside down. My mind tries to reason with what I'm seeing. Finally, the shapes and details become more solid.

The Hurricane is resting on its passenger side. Above us, as if in a spaceship with no gravity, Margret struggles with her seatbelt. "We might catch on fire. We have to get everyone out of here. Quickly."

"How?" I look toward the front and see Ron and Susan are both unconscious. Or worse. There's only me and one frail senior to lift them all out. I stand up now, tippy-toe to reach the door, the one in the air. The one at

Margret's side. My fingers barely touch. "I can't slide the door open from this distance."

"Hmm. Let me try." She pushes the unlock button, then heaves the sliding door to one side. None of this part of the Hurricane seems to be damaged.

"Now how do I get up?" I ask, looking around for things to climb on.

"Scootch over a bit," she tells me.

I squeeze tightly against the front seat as Margret's seat buckle gives.

She rolls down to the floor beside me, half on top of me. "Uh!" Then she slowly straightens. "Here!" she cups her hands. "Step up and I'll give you a boost."

I take a deep breath and stand on her bony inter-locked fingers.

"Okay, this works."

"Now climb out," Margret tells me.

"Really? Then what? You gonna lift Linda to me?"

"Maybe I won't have to. Start with Ron. Try to wake him up."

I spring up from her cupped hands and climb toward the driver's side of the car, grabbing the handle. I pull the door open but gravity works against me, the door wants to shut again. Quickly, I wedge myself so it can't. The door crashes against my back. Uh! I lean over and call softly near his ear, "Ron, Ron! Wake up. I need your help." If he can't move on his own, I don't see how Margret and I can lift him.

He moans, but when his eyes open, I warn him, "I'm going to release your seatbelt. Grab hold of my shoulder and hoist yourself out." He doesn't answer. "Can you do that?" I repeat.

He takes a few moments and groans as his left arm drops. "I think my wrist is broken." With only his right hand gripping my shoulder, I reach my arms around him and pull. His fingers dig in but he's a dead weight. I can't budge him.

"Can you push off of your feet?"

"Uhh." He groans again. "They don't work!" Instead, he digs his elbows into the car door to move himself along while I lean back. Bit by bit, he lifts out.

Finally, when we're at the edge of the SUV, I jump down and try to catch him as he tumbles over the side. It's all I can do. His legs won't hold him.

"We need to get you farther away from the car. Can you roll yourself?" I ask him.

Ron doesn't answer — can't; he's passed out. I reach under his armpits and try to drag him. I can't budge him.

"Linda's next!" Margret calls and I know I have to leave him.

Stepping onto a tire, I reach to grip a pipe and hoist myself back up. The car wobbles. Will it fall over on top of me? I wait for a moment.

No?

Good.

By the time I make it back to the door, Linda has already come to and Margret is struggling to boost her up. Who would have thought Margret could be so strong? I grab Linda the same way I did Ron. But she's lighter, maybe less hurt, definitely way easier. Gently, gently we make it to the cliff of the car. I jump to the ground and she follows, with me cushioning her as best I can. She stumbles alongside of me and I set her down near Ron.

Now there's only Margret and Susan. Smoke rises from the engine as I climb more quickly back up the side of the SUV.

Okay, this time it definitely teeters. *Easy*, I tell myself. "Ready!" I call to Margret. "Get Susan up here."

"I keep calling her. She won't wake up," Margret says. Kneeling on the door and bent sideways over her, Margret puts two fingers to Susan's neck. After a moment, she shakes her head ... no, nothing, answering a question no one has dared to ask. She pulls back and covers her own face with a hand.

"She's not dead!"

Margret starts to cry.

"She can't be!" I jump down through the door. Landing, I collide with her. "Come on." I touch her shoulder. "Let's get you out."

She cries harder. But I lace my fingers and bend down. "You have to go now! Hurry!" Can a person this age climb out and get to the ground by herself? I frown as I look at her crumpled face. She has to try. "Come on!"

She steps on my hands, holding on to my shoulder. Up, up. She's going to make it. She falls against the side of the Hurricane and I feel it shake.

But I can't worry about that now. I reach around the seat to check Susan. No matter where my fingers touch her, there's no answering beat. I put my face close to her mouth; there's no breath.

I happen to see the El-Q lying on the floor and I squeeze between the two seats, crawling and reaching to pick it up. I tap the button to summon Genie and shout to her. "Find me CPR Instructions!" Then I manoeuvre myself to stand on the door nearest Susan and hit the lever at the side of her seat to fold it down flat.

The computer voice answers almost immediately, *Here's what I found on the web for CPR instructions.*

I check the screen and tap on the video. Then I tap up the volume.

As it plays and the instructions are given, I open Susan's coat.

Find the breastbone in the centre of the victim's chest.

I follow along, placing my hands the way the instructor says, interlacing my fingers. Then I pump. Hard enough? Did I break a rib? Was that two inches? It's her only chance, so who cares, I do it again. And again.

Thirty times. "She's not going to die," I shout as I push down. Eli has to hear me, wherever he is. "That wasn't the agreement."

The SUV wobbles as Margret's head appears in the window. "You have to get out now. The engine's on fire."

From somewhere in the distance, I hear the mosquito whine of a siren.

"I can't leave her." I shake my head. A cold realization hits me as I watch the El-Q video. What was it that Eli told me when we first met? That my cellphone would kill me. Genie found these website instructions and they're what keeps me in this SUV attempting to restart Susan's heart.

I keep pumping, understanding what he means to do. "Really, Eli? This is the new ending you want to give us? Bring it on!"

The mosquito whine grows louder now and is joined by another and another. Sirens suddenly howl from all directions.

Then just as suddenly, the loudest stops. The SUV rocks wildly and a face appears in that door in the air. A hand reaches down to me. "Time to go!" a voice calls.

I lean my head to Susan's chest but can't make out whether it's an answering pulse I feel or the thrum from the sirens. I shake my head. "I can't tell if I have a heartbeat yet."

"We'll take over now."

I reach toward the hand and grab hold. Up and over I scramble.

There's a lightning flash and a scream of white pain in my head. I fall to the ground and have to concentrate on just breathing through it all for a moment.

"Move her out of here. Now!"

Someone lifts my arm and tucks himself under, lifting me, dragging me, roughly.

Ow, ow, ow! Every footstep reverberates through my bones and brain. Finally, I slide from the bulky shoulder, hit the dirt hard.

In that moment, the ground shudders. I feel a blast of heat and hear a roar.

Everything goes dark.

CHAPTER 32

Hallie

THIS PLACE ISN'T HALF BAD. The sunlight streaming through the skylights warms my face and feels heavenly, the promise of spring in January and all that. Windows everywhere make the open space bright. A hint of cinnamon hangs in the air; someone must be baking, maybe in the crafts room.

A soft ding signals an elevator arrival. From my seat in this foyer, I look over toward it and see the door slide open. A wheelchair rolls forward and I know she has arrived.

Susan smiles and waves, then pushes Ron in the chair toward us.

I wave back.

Ron's right hand lifts from the arm rest, a bit of a finger wave. No cast on his wrist today, which fractured when the airbag blew his hand against the window. He still has casts on both of his legs. When the Hurricane hit the concrete guardrail, his side at the front took the brunt of it.

Susan looks way better than he does. No major injury from the accident, just a continued failing heart. On our last El-Q Hangout, she told me if she were just a few years younger, she would sign up for a transplant.

Sitting at my side, Hardeep raises his eyebrows. He's brought a large ball of pale green wool with a couple of metal needles poking through. He's planning to make a scarf for his new baby niece.

Seated next to him, Abby holds a ball of indigo-coloured wool that picks up the colour of her hair. She's hoping to knit a beret.

They're both pretty ambitious. I have leftovers from Mom's crocheting days. Candy-apple red and magenta yarn, which I'm aiming to make a square with, maybe to use as a potholder, probably just to keep as a practice souvenir — remembering your first project kind-of-thing.

As Susan and Ron draw nearer, I can see a floral-patterned knitting bag resting in Ron's lap. This will be good therapy for his hand. That's what Susan says, anyway. She bought the wool to make Leah the mittens she asked for, and she's hoping for Ron's help.

He's expected to make a full recovery, only slower than Mr. Impatience wants. Plenty of time to make one half of the pair, Susan thinks. Meantime, he doesn't want Sheryl giving him personal care. Well, Susan suspects it really was the other way around. Ron told her they were having difficulties even before the accident.

So Ron became Susan's excuse. She moved into Elmwood Village to keep him company. Still Ron won't be in Elmwood forever, just till he can look after himself.

"Hi, how are you?" I ask them both.

Before they can answer, Gord runs in with a tray of buns. The cinnamon smell grows stronger. Too funny, he's the baker. He grins. "You need something to eat when you work!"

Knitting is work? For Gordon, maybe. I'm pretty sure he only does it so he can hang around Susan.

She smiles. "I've gained ten pounds this month. You have to stop!" She takes a bun, inhales, and bites in. "Mmmm!"

Gord's ploy seems to be working. He's definitely winning Susan over, and it's another reason for her to hate the move to the residence a little less.

I take a cinnamon bun, too. Still warm, slightly gooey, with soft white icing that sticks to everything. That'll delay our start for sure; we'll have to wash our fingers. Very fattening, too, but who cares. I sink my teeth in. "Mmmm."

It's been a long month. I missed Christmas day, at least the actual date, but my family saved unwrapping all the presents for when I got out of the hospital a week later. Christmas and New Year's all rolled into one. We ate Chinese food. It was the best ever, even though I had some whopper headaches. A concussion. Bouncing my skull off a car window will do that.

Every ornament shone brighter than before, the colours of the tree and ribbons and presents pulsed at me, they were so vivid. Mom and Dad bought me some sneakers I had been begging for and gave me money. Maybe I could put it toward driving lessons. I don't know anymore. I didn't care about the presents. I was just happy to be there with my family. We all sat around watching *The Sound of Music* together. We sang "Edelweiss." I cried.

I smile now, remembering it all.

"This is delicious," Hardeep says about his cinnamon bun as he digs in.

Somehow he manages to get a dab of white icing on his cheek, and when he grins, it's so little kid, I can't help grinning, too. I also can't resist touching his face. Then I gently wipe the icing away with a napkin. I can count on Hardeep to help me with whatever I'm doing. Research on Saji Motors, knitting with the golden oldies, practicing a goal kick. And under that Union Jack cap of his, he has this great glossy black hair.

"Thanks. Glad you're enjoying it," Gord answers.

For a while the only sounds are more moans over how tasty the fresh baked treats are.

Then Ron straightens in his chair. "I have good news."

For a moment I almost expect him to get up and walk. That would probably be the best news. I put my cinnamon bun down.

"Saji Motors has offered us a settlement."

"Yay!" I cheer and clap. The others join in, too.

"So we don't have to collect more names for a class-action suit?" Hardeep asks. "'Cause a tow truck driver from Saji Motors just stepped forward. He has a bunch of possible names for us."

"Oh no. You keep up that website and message board. They want to pay us a hundred thousand dollars so we will sign off and leave them alone."

"That's a lot of money," Susan says. "Are we really going to turn that down?"

"Small potatoes! We need big figures to attract the public's attention. No corporation should ever want to risk our safety for profit again." He bites into his cinnamon bun and Susan wipes the icing from his mouth with a napkin.

"Mom, really, I can do it myself."

"Of course you can, darling."

I can't help smiling. Nice to see the mom treating her son like a kid instead of the other way around.

Suddenly, Margret bustles in. "Stupid bus system. Takes forever to get here on public transit."

"You know the answer to that one. Just move here, too," Susan says.

"I put my name on the waiting list!" Linda says, following on her heels. She looks great in her red coat and fuchsia pants. Bright and colourful, no after-effects at all from the accident.

Margret sets down her large bag and hangs up her coat. Then she spies the cinnamon buns and grabs one. "You're all going to have to wash your hands before you touch your knitting needles!"

"No problem," I say. My El-Q burps. Megan texting? I reach for it and then pull back. My fingers are too sticky. And anyhow, Eli's wrong, I'm not addicted. Watch how I leave the El-Q alone. We'll be meeting Megan later at the library for the Teen-Senior Technology session, anyway. It's the new program we developed with Burlington Public Library. Fully booked for this first session. Chael and Kendra signed up, too. Everyone needs those volunteer hours, after all.

Too bad Eli doesn't come. He could see that cellphones don't have to kill anyone; they can connect all these seniors to their families around the world. And they can video a bad car accident and prove that a gas pedal is sticky. I lick my fingers clean and reach forward again. Maybe I better check that text anyway, just in case Megan has to cancel for some reason.

It's not from any number I recognize. But the message is familiar. *Get off the phone. Carpe Diem.*

Eli.

ACKNOWLEDGEMENTS

THANK YOU TO THE ONTARIO ARTS COUNCIL for the financial support.

It takes a lot of experts to make things go wrong enough for a story to happen.

A huge thank you to Todd Sarson, Service Manager at Stop N Go Automotive, for assisting me with the faulty accelerator issues. Another big thank you to Constable Chantelle Wilson for helping me navigate police procedure for the best story outcome. Mistakes that happened despite their assistance, I embrace (and celebrate!) as my own.

Thank you to Burlington Public Library for all their support and their special Teen/Senior Tech meet-up. For camaraderie and support, CANSCAIP and the Writers' Union of Canada are always there for me.

To all the writers who listened and contributed their thoughts, friendship, and cookies: Gisela Sherman, Lynda Simmons, Rachael Preston, Rebecca Bender, Lana Button, Gillian Chan, Vicki Grant, Jennifer Maruno, Jennifer Mook-Sang, Mahtab Narsimhan, Judith Robinson, Susanne Del Rizzo, Claudia White, Rory D'Eon, Janice D'Eon, Chelsea

Rainford, Steve Donnelly, Jim Bennett, Judy Glen, and Amy Corbin — my sincerest gratitude.

Thank you to my agent David Bennett who loves my writing even more than my mother did.

Finally, cheers and hugs to the outstanding team at Dundurn for their hard work in getting this book into your hands.